Henry & Eva

and the CASTLE ON THE CLIFF

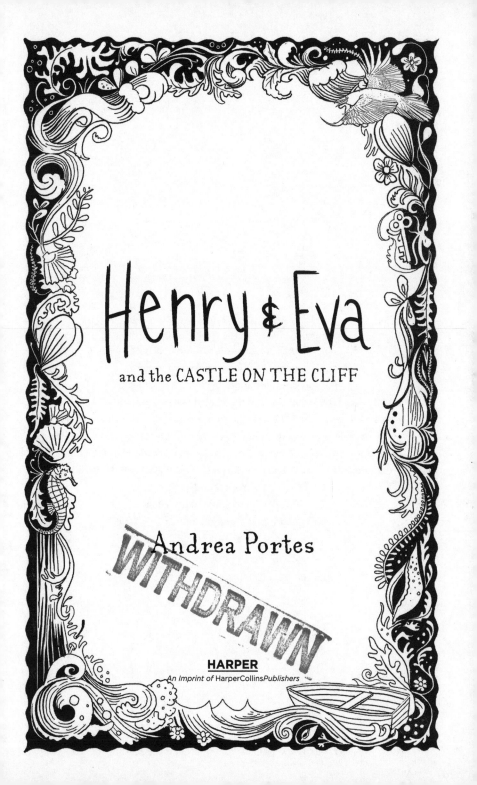

Henry & Eva

and the CASTLE ON THE CLIFF

Andrea Portes

WITHDRAWN

HARPER

An Imprint of HarperCollinsPublishers

For Wyatt.

You are my everything.

There are more things in heaven and earth, Horatio,

Than are dreamt of in your philosophy.

—William Shakespeare, *Hamlet* (1.5.167–8)

PART ONE

1

SOMETIMES THINGS CAN be perfect. Sometimes everything and everyone you know can just float around in a kind of eternal, blissful loop like nothing can ever change and the world will just keep spinning perfectly on its axis, giggling, delirious with each turn.

And sometimes it can all fall apart.

Just like that.

SMASH.

Shards everywhere, sharp like a room full of razors.

Faster than you can say "Wait, but I didn't know it would go! Hold on! I didn't know it could ever change" it does change. And by then it's too late.

Here. I'll show you.

Look over there. See that gray stone fence that looks like it's been here since before Columbus discovered America? The one covered with vines? Under the vines, the gray stones peeking out, playing hide-and-seek. Okay, now through that gate, the black, wrought-iron one.

There, see the big thicket full of trees? Eucalyptus, Torrey pines, cypresses, and even some redwoods? Okay, now down that dirt road. Through the clover and watch out for the poison oak.

There's the clearing.

The light coming through the edge of the trees.

This is the part where I always have to stop. To catch my breath. To take it in. To feel it again for the thousandth time just like the first time.

Look.

The grass meadow swooping down down down into the cliffs and there, beyond the cliffs, the crashing deep blue Pacific Ocean. Westward, young one. That's the direction you face. If you were magic you could see all the way to Tokyo.

And there, just where the meadow starts to swoop upward, perched just before the cliffs, the old Victorian house that looks a lot like it's haunted. Yes, people think it's a haunted house, but I know it's not because it's *my* house.

I think it's the spires that make it look like a natural ghost habitat. And the wraparound porch. And the turrets. And the tiny graveyard in the corner of the property. That usually clinches it for people. But it's been there forever. I mean, what are we gonna do? Move it?

See that little boy there? On the steps of the porch, looking out at the ocean? Well, that little boy there with the dark hair and giant eyes . . . that's Henry. My kid brother. And, if it were two months ago, my kid brother Henry would come running up to me, and we'd go play hide-and-seek, or leapfrog, or we'd build an ant farm, or fashion a kite out of sticks and leaves, or we'd race all the way down the craggy path to the tiny beach below and throw ourselves onto the sand, panting, trying to catch our breath.

But it's not two months ago.

It's now.

Two months after our parents died.

2

WHEN YOU SEE it in the newspaper it looks like this:

PROMINENT ENVIRONMENTALIST AND OCEANOGRAPHER DIE IN BOATING ACCIDENT

BIG SUR—Prominent environmentalist William Billings (43) and his oceanographer wife, Margo (39), died in a boating accident off the coast of Moss Landing. A police spokeswoman said the couple died when their boat turned over in the Portuguese Ledge State Marine Conservation area, during a sudden storm. William Billings was vice president of the Northern California Conservation Society and a board member of numerous environmental

protection groups. He received the National Environmental Leadership Award for his work preserving the California coastline. Margo Billings, widely credited with the reinvigoration of Monterey Bay, was president of the Marine Mammal Preservation Cooperative. The couple leaves behind a twelve-year-old daughter and a ten-year-old son.

It doesn't say I remember what she was wearing that day. She was wearing a navy-and-white-striped shirt and we joked around that she looked like a sailor and should be wearing a captain's hat. It doesn't say Henry thought they should bring sandwiches but Mom said she wasn't hungry and so Henry made her just take some dried nectarines. It doesn't say Dad had SPF 50 sunscreen all over his face and he looked like a ghost so I rubbed it in and he said "Boo!" and smiled and he tried to tickle me but I rolled my eyes and told him, Dad, I'm too old for tickling.

It says that I am twelve and that Henry is ten but it doesn't say that Henry will be eleven in three months and we were already starting to plan his birthday party. It was going to be a spooky birthday party because Henry loves spooky things, especially skeleton pirates, and his birthday is October 26, so every year we have a "Spooky Birthday Party Spectacular" including a disco haunted house with glow sticks and a skull piñata.

It doesn't say that now we will not be having that party because all Henry can do is sit on those steps and look out at the ocean and wait for my mom and my dad to come home.

And that would be a sad but peaceful thing to do, except . . .

"Would you kids stop making all that racket!"

That's Terri. We call her "Terri the Terrible."

Terri the Terrible is here to take care of us. Along with Claude, our uncle. We have also nicknamed Claude: "Claude the Clod." So, between Terri the Terrible and Claude the Clod it's a mouthful, but we kind of need it to get through, because, well, because they are jerk-faces. First class, grade A.

When we found out they were coming to take care of us we practically hurled ourselves off the cliff.

I know, *I know*, I'm supposed to be nice. But listen to this. The first day Terri the Terrible came in here, the first thing she did was move all the mahogany and cherrywood furniture up to the attic and replace it with a bunch of fake-royal, gold-gilded garbage that my mom would have thrown in the Dumpster before feeling guilty and then giving it to Goodwill. I'm serious. Everything in here is gold now and it makes no sense. This is a hundred-and-sixty-year-old house with wood everywhere and creaky stairs and now everything in here looks like it belongs on some kind of game show or reality TV program about housewives.

Terri wasn't even nice about it. And she was mean to the guys. The guys moving it. She didn't even treat them like people.

That's the other thing.

Mom and Dad were always super nice to anyone who came

in to do anything here in our place. As long as I can remember they would drill into us that everybody was equal and that we should treat everyone with respect, see what we could learn from those around us, and ask questions. It was common decency, Mom said. And if someone needed something, we should bend over backward to help them.

Helping other people was an *opportunity* to be a better person, Dad told us.

Their philosophy was simple, really. Their philosophy was kindness.

Not Terri's.

She didn't even look at the movers when she told them where to put all her horrible stuff. She just barked.

She even saw me looking at her in disbelief. You know how she replied?

"Oh, honey. I know it seems harsh; you can't let these people take advantage of you."

These people.

I think I know what she means by that.

Anyone else would have been mortified, but Terri didn't seem to care. She just kept on barking orders and checking herself in that gold-gilded mirror and clinking the ice in her glass.

That's something she's really good at. Ice-clinking. Pouring lots and lots of liquid into a glass, swirling and clinking that ice in that glass some more.

And the worst part? She smokes.

I told her no one is allowed to smoke in our

one-hundred-and-sixty-year-old house because it's a fire haz-ard and, also, it's gross, but she said, "There's new rules now, sweetie." And that was that.

And Claude the Clod? Well, he's here but he's not *here*. He's never really anywhere. He's kind of got his phone, or his Bluetooth, constantly glued to his ear and there is always an important phone call and he always has to get it no matter what. He has so many important phone calls you'd think he was the president of the world.

It's always *blah blah blah* land deal or *yadda yadda* leases or *whoop de doo* tenants or permits or condos. Yep, he's a real go-getter. If you want to engage him, better talk about real estate, because that's all he cares about. One time he talked to me for an hour about the rise in market value of a Taco Bell near the Ontario airport.

Claude, I get the feeling, is the kind of person who could be vacationing in Rome and gaze up at the most beautiful cathe-dral, temple, or museum on earth and he would just say, "I wonder how much this place goes for?"

In case you are wondering, we do have another uncle . . . a long-lost uncle named Finn. Nobody has seen him for years because he's too busy hiking the Himalayas or living among the Inuit people of the Arctic Circle or something. There's a pic-ture of him on the fireplace mantle, his face sunburned and lips chapped, smiling a toothy grin next to a Sherpa on the second base camp of Mount Everest. Although I have high hopes for him as a person of fascination and intrigue, I have zero hopes for him as someone who could actually take care of me and Henry in this particular domestic situation. Other than this photo, I've seen neither hide nor hair of Uncle Finn throughout the twelve years of my life thus far.

So, well . . . he's out of the question.

We're left with Clod and Terrible.

I can't wrap my head around it. My mom and dad were so busy thinking about the oceans rising and the sun blazing, but somehow they never thought of *this*. A plan for us. Right here at home. In case something horrible happened. And then something horrible happened.

Sometimes I look at Terri and Claude and I think, *Maybe Mom and Dad knew something we didn't. Maybe they're not so bad after all?*

"Why do you kids insist on making so much noise?"

There she goes again. Standing in front of me and Henry on the stairs, she turns to me.

"Sweetie, you should really dye that hair. You look like a mouse! But the good news is mouse-brown hair goes to blond so easy. Just look at me!"

Henry looks at me and I try to freeze my face.

I do not say, "You mean, I would be pretty like you if I had banana-yellow hair and black roots and jewelry all over the place and makeup that looks like I've been applying and reapplying it for five hours straight?"

Everything about Terri feels so . . . fake. Right down to the baubles she has dangling on every available limb.

That's the other thing. My mom never really wore jewelry. I mean, if it was a night out, she'd put on maybe a bracelet. But it would be an embroidered bracelet. From Istanbul. The kind of thing you wouldn't notice at first and then you *would* notice it and realize it was the most intricate thing you ever saw. She didn't care about diamonds or sparkly things that cost a zillion dollars because the things she thought were beautiful were things that came splashing out of the sea, things that played in the wake of a boat and talked to each other in whistles and clicks and underwater songs.

And makeup wasn't at the top of her to-do list, either. Well, maybe if she felt like it, but even then just a little lipstick and mascara. Something subtle but not too committed. She would ask my dad, "Does this lipstick make me look like I'm trying too hard and everyone should fall in love with me because I'm pathetically desperate?" And my dad would shake his head.

Wow. Did he love her. She was always so strange, and her train of thought always went off in the funniest directions, and you couldn't help but laugh at the weird, goofy, absurd paths her brain would take.

But makeup was never the focus of those strange musings.

So, you see, she was basically the opposite of Terri the Terrible.

I have a funny memory of my dad and mom having a "discussion" about having to spend Thanksgiving with Uncle Claude and Aunt Terri one year. It went something like this:

"Honey, husband, love of my life. I know that family is a priority, but maybe you could just send your brother and his girlfriend a fruit basket and we can go to West Marin? I mean, it's not like you ever see him. Or talk to him. Or go bicycling with him down the coast and have a picnic and start singing that song from *The Sound of Music* in rounds with each other."

"Margo, I understand that you're not excited to go down to Orange County for Thanksgiving, but—"

"William Alexander Billings. It's not that I'm not excited. It's that I think I would rather slather myself in meat and frosting and throw myself in a great white shark breeding ground at sunset."

"Why at sunset?"

"Feeding time."

He nods.

"Margo Elizabeth Billings, maiden name Burke. If you slathered yourself in meat and frosting and went into a great white shark breeding ground at sunset then I would slather myself in *even more* meat and frosting and jump in before you. So, fine. We won't go."

"YAY! Let's take the kids to West Marin, but don't tell them, let's keep it a surprise!"

She was always doing that. Surprises. It filled her with glee. Silly things. Ugly Christmas sweaters. A spooky bounce house. A Cinco de Mayo party in the middle of March, because March is so boring. After-dinner Mexican Loteria. A Chinese firework display on a random Wednesday night. A piñata for no apparent reason. She loved that stuff. Celebrations. Decorations. Surprises.

But the last surprise was not a happy surprise.

That would have really irked her.

At night, lying awake with the moon coming in through the blinds' wooden slats, I see her. My mother, floating down down down into the sea, the moonlight in shards streaking through the water, her hair floating up above her, swaying gently back and forth, in the current, and around her, all around her, they come. The dolphins. And the whales. And the seals and sea otters. They all come to thank her. To honor her for honoring them. And they escort her, gently, gently down to her bed at the bottom of the sea. And they tuck her in, a blanket of silt, and surround her in a quiet prayer. We will protect you. We will comfort you. We will watch over you. And I wake up from this dream, each time, and look over at my little brother, because I have to make sure he can't hear me cry.

3

TONIGHT IS TERRI the Terrible's big night. She is hosting her first soiree. It will be her big opportunity to show everyone the new kid in town—herself!

Henry and I are in charge of greeting her guests and getting their coats.

Marisol, our part-of-the-family-and-ever-beloved nanny, is supposed to relieve us of our coat-getting duty and then ferret us away so we can't ruin the party. Because Terri says she doesn't want a bunch of "screaming kids" around.

As if.

Fun fact: Marisol is the only one left around here who cares about us. She tucks us into bed and reads us stories and plays with us and helps us with our school projects and last night we even made homemade playdough. She told us you could even eat it, if you were hungry. But it would mostly just taste like eating purple.

Marisolita Ana Maria Zeron, aka Marisol, is from Guatemala and we basically all speak Spanglish to each other. My dad speaks . . . *spoke* fluent Spanish, from all this research he did in South America before he met my mom, so he and Marisol could talk and talk. He loved it. My mom used to tease him and call him a show-off, but I think she just wished she could speak it, too.

Henry and I know a few songs she taught us. *"La Itzi Bitzi Araña"* ("The Itsy Bitsy Spider") and *"La Cucaracha"* ("The Cockroach") and *"Mariquita Mariquita"* ("Ladybug, Ladybug").

Come to think of it, all the songs are insect related. Is that weird?

But, yeah, we know some Español. We couldn't have a conversation about the meaning of life, or supply-side economics, or anything. But we get by.

Marisol is really pretty, you know. She has giant brown eyes and a round face and long black hair that just goes straight no matter what. But what makes her really pretty is that she kind of just shines. Like there's this glow around her. Made of kindness or something. And she loves us. She really does.

Since the accident, Henry has had a really hard time sleeping unless she's right there beside us. He wakes up crying sometimes and calls for her. She always comes in. Even though her bedroom is down the hall.

I think Marisol feels like we're her kids, kinda. She was young when she came here and she's been with us the whole time. She never talks about what it was like to get here in the first place. From Guatemala. But I heard my mom talking to her about it once and, even just from talking about it, my mom started crying. Right there at the kitchen table. Marisol didn't cry, though. It was like she wouldn't let herself. Or maybe she couldn't.

And I am thankful for her every day.

Especially now.

"Um, Uncle Claude? Who exactly is coming to this party?"

He's on his phone. Of course.

The caterers and bartender are walking back and forth through the house like it's the train station. Terri the Terrible had wanted me to help her invite every one of my mom's friends and donors.

I *might* have told her I didn't know how to get ahold of them.

I *might not* have admitted I have been collecting the invites to every charitable event from Mendocino to Monterey that have been appearing in the mailbox for my mom, who is now dead, each day for the past two months.

I might also have left out that I have a secret shoe box of all those invites hidden away.

Let her build her own mailing list. This one is my mother's, and she earned it.

"Hmm?" Claude sort of answers.

"Who's coming to this party?"

"Huh? I don't know. Business associates?"

"Sounds . . . fun."

He nods. I guess he doesn't get my sense of humor.

Henry and I look at each other.

"Oooo. I have an idea," I say. "Let's play Boring People Bingo."

This is a great game. My mom made it up. What you do is this: If you know you're going to be spending time with a person, or a group of people, who always talks about the same boring things, you make a bingo chart. You can make up things to put in the squares like "Real Estate Purchase" or "Cost of Something" or "Random New Diet." You just fill in all the squares in the chart. Then you keep that little chart next to you, or near you, and you tally it up the whole night. You have to play it with someone, though. It's no fun on your own. Whoever fills in all the squares first wins.

"C'mon, Henry. You know you want to."

He looks at me. He doesn't smile. He really doesn't smile much these days.

In fact, my job, and I take it very seriously, is to cheer up my brother. This usually involves dance numbers. Also, songs.

I like to make up songs about whatever is going on around us and perform them that evening to rousing applause from Marisol and a roll of the eyes from Henry. But a roll of the eyes is better than nothing and I know I am closing in on a smile soon. I can feel it.

Tonight, the cheering-up concept is Boring People Bingo.

"Pleeeeeeease? Please, Henry? It's no fun without you."

"Aaaaall right."

I jump up and down, clapping. I know this will compensate, if only momentarily, for Terri the Terrible's gold-gilded, people-impressing extravaganza.

"Eva, sweetie, can you please go out and close the gate to the path? I don't want anyone falling off the cliff tonight."

Ugh. Terri always has a list of things for me to do. It's okay, though. Might be nice to get some fresh air before the Business Associates' Ball.

There's a little wooden gate you have to unhitch to get onto the path down the craggy rocks, which leads you to the beach below. The beach is a little sliver at the bottom of the cliffs. Just a tiny strip. At high tide it's about eleven feet wide. At low tide it's about eighteen feet. Narrow enough that nobody would want to hang out down there for fear of the tide or a rogue wave swooping them into the sea.

From the gate you can barely see down the slippery rock path to the water, but tonight is the full moon, reflected off the water like a squiggling line going straight up the beach to the moon. We've lived here all my life but it still stops my breath every time I see it. That giant white moon over the tumbling sea and the cliffs. It feels like looking at heaven. Like for a moment, we get to see it.

I'm just about to turn and go back to make my Boring People Bingo charts when I spy something strange.

Down on the water, through the jagged rocks and the brambles.

There, down there. I see it.

Next to the water. Coming out of the water.

There.

Do you see it?

Hovering there over the waves?

4

THE MIST ABOVE the waves is dividing itself in fractals and spinning forms, whipping around and then disappearing into the air. The fog makes nautilus shell patterns swirling *up up up* into the moonlit night. Circular trails into the stars above.

I've lived here my entire life, was brought here the day after I was born, and have never seen a thing like this before. Not even on a science show. *Discover. Planet Earth. National Geographic.* I watch them all.

And then it makes a sound. "It" being the indescribable, intangible, and probably imaginary spinning vortex before me above the shore.

FSHHHHHHHHHH.

Fshhhhhh.

FSHHHHHHHHHHhhhhhhh.

Needless to say, the alphabet leaves a lot to be desired in terms of describing the aforementioned sound. Imagine the sound of a hurricane coupled with a friendly snake—a kind of whistling wind crossed with swirling maraca.

Here is the bizarre thing: For all intents and purposes, this swirling vortex sighting, accompanied by this otherworldly sound, should be terrifying. Yet it's not. Instead, it hovers there, spinning out of the water and into the breeze, a luminous lavender whirling—whispering, with a kind of inviting warmth.

The moon behind is nearly full, low in the sky, casting phantom squiggles on the ocean in shimmering light. Beside me, the jagged cliffs hurl themselves up to the stars like black and gray skyscrapers.

This next part is going to make it sound like I lost my marbles somewhere in the northern Pacific, but there is really no way to spill the beans here unless I just admit it.

I feel the *presence of something* . . . something familiar in the middle of this myriad of spinning light and shadows.

I feel the presence of something sparkling and majestic, a kind of churning mischief. A kind of sheltering.

As if at any moment it will appear.

It will appear and carry me gently away with it.

So I do the only thing I can.

"HENRY!!!" I scream, and I tear up the rock path to the gate.

5

THE PARTY IS now going on up the cliffs; I can hear the clink of glasses and the sound of polite laughter wafting out the windows and through the air up into the night sky. The windows, glowing orange squares, beckon me from the green salt air below.

There is only one thing to do.

Find Henry.

Over the sloping grass, up the wooden porch, through the entry hall smothered in coats and hats, I catapult myself into the mahogany ballroom. There, at the other end of the hall, is Henry.

He is doing a magic trick.

Fun fact: Four years ago, Mom hired a magician for my

birthday party and, ever since then, you might as well call Henry "The Great Houdini." At first, the tricks were pretty pathetic, but he was six and it was so adorable and nobody minded. But then he got pretty good at about ten tricks, tricks he mastered, tricks he spent *hours* going over and over in his bedroom, until one day, he emerged, the Great Henrini.

Right now he is doing a trick involving a fake rabbit, a black box, and a rubber chicken. He turns the rabbit into a chicken. Everyone oohs and aahs. Then, he turns the chicken back into the rabbit. Everyone freaks out.

It's a solid trick. (It used to be his closer.)

Even though I am hyperventilating and need to get him down to the beach to see . . . whatever that is, I cannot bear to ruin his Great Henrini Magic.

This is the first time he's done his routine since the accident.

I watch him, proud and a little bit wistful.

"Ladies and gentlemen, I give you . . ."

He takes out the now-transformed rubber chicken.

"A chicken!"

The crowd of dressed-up but not-too-dressed-up adults applauds, wineglasses in hand.

"Oh, but, wait. I forgot something. Hold on one second. I meant to say . . . I give you a . . . BUNNY RABBIT!"

Gasps. Exclamations. Anarchy.

The dazzled adults clap enthusiastically, some of them even putting down their wineglasses to do it. (You know it's important when adults put down their wine. Especially here, in California wine country, where everyone is always talking about hints of berry and a slight peppery aroma and whether a certain vintage is "long on the tongue." I mean, they really push the boundaries of acceptable things to say without bursting into laughter.)

I have a flash of my dad imitating someone quite self-serious, nose-raised and pretentious, on the way back from a Christmas party in Pebble Beach. "Yes, yes, I detect hints of paprika. And . . . on the back of the tongue . . . lingonberry? Or perhaps the third egg of a Tasmanian sea turtle. But just a hint!" Now, in this memory, my mom laughs and joins in. "Peaches! Yes, yes, plums! Five grains of sand from the Tunisian desert!" Now we are all doing it. "Sandwiches! Pencil shavings, thatches from a roof in Bali!" Even sleepy Henry joins in: "The bishop off a chessboard carved in Bulgaria! No, wait . . . Latvia!" We are all driving down the coast, cracking each other up, spouting more and more random things, in voices that, basically, start as sort of snooty then devolve into something strangely reptilian. We are just making each other laugh with our absurd lizard voices.

My dad was gasping for air. He actually had to pull the car over so he wouldn't crash. I bet we looked ridiculous, a car full of people by the side of the road, guffawing uncontrollably. We'd catch our breath, there would be a lull, and another explosion. Trying not to laugh, laughing at each other's laughs. Contagious.

I think of that moment as Henry completes his last and final trick: the Disappearing Flaming Candelabra. It's a real humdinger. Abracadabra, light the match, presto chango, and the entire ballroom explodes in applause. Ecstatic clapping. *Ecstatic.* Straight up the beadboard walls, over the oil paintings of long-dead ancestors, and high above into the rafters. *Clap clap clap.*

Looks like they got their money's worth. Not that anyone paid to be here. But who knows what they were expecting? Most of them have never been here before, these friends of Claude the Clod and Terri the Terrible. The guys wear gray pants and light blue button-down shirts, the uniform, and their wives are all a bit younger than they would be, say, in a normal place. A bit curvier. And again with the jewelry. This is the most gold jewelry this house has ever seen.

But they're nice enough, and the fact that they seem to adore Henry makes me like them a little bit, actually.

Then Terri the Terrible approaches.

"What a *lovely* magic show!" she trumpets to the room.

"I'm glad you liked it," she whispers to a woman to her right.

"Well, isn't he just a hit!!" She gives the next gentleman a jolly little slap on the bicep.

She looks around the room, drinking in the success of her first event.

Claude is over in the corner, surrounded by light blue shirts, regaling them with the story of the first time he paved paradise and put up a parking lot. They are all ears. It's his party, after all. He is allowed all the real estate talk he can muster.

Me? I need to get out of here. "Excuse me, Terri. Great party!"

"Yes, it is. And isn't it also time for you to *scurry along to bed*?"

She narrows her eyes at me almost imperceptibly.

"Yup. Scurrying." I shuffle through the crowd to find the Great Henrini, who is packing up his magic accoutrement.

I smile and talk through my gritted teeth. "Henry, you have to come with me. Right now!"

"I kind of blew the three-ring trick—"

"Henry, put that stuff down, you're never gonna believe what is—"

"The ring got stuck, so you could sort of tell—" He's mostly talking to himself. "It was a little embarrassing, actually."

"Okay, stop talking. Listen to me. There is some kind of supernatural slash meteorological event happening down the cliffs and—"

Now he stops putting everything into his mystical black suitcase.

"What?"

"You have to see. Levitating fractals. Or paranormal phenomenon. Or maybe both."

The mystical black suitcase falls to the floor.

6

LOOK. THEY SORT of didn't know what to do with him, my brother. In school, they'd be going on and on about London Bridge falling down, and he'd be over in the corner somewhere building a ten-foot model of that very same bridge out of shoe boxes.

That's the way it is with Henry. You look over at him, have a five-minute conversation with someone, look back and he's created a mile-long marble run. And there he would be still squinting into his work. Adjusting.

Is that the Sistine Chapel made of stuffed animals, you'd ask? Yup, and there would be Henry, placing his oldest teddy bear as the keystone. Henry is always constructing. Always perfecting. In silence. It's just how his mind works. Engineering.

Experimenting. That's where he lives. In those little worlds he makes.

But they thought there was something wrong with him. Because he wasn't interested in making eye contact. Or in human interaction in general. Or most of the trivialities of everyday interfacing. He just wanted to get back to his robot laboratory or his flying-car factory or his potion-concocting mill.

Not that other stuff. Not that playdate nonsense.

And so they made us test him. When he was six. And the test came back that he had an IQ of 180. And there was a word they used. The doctors. High-functioning something-or-other. Profound whatchamacallit. There's a lot of words for it, I guess.

Our word for it was Henry.

They wanted us to continue, the institute. They hoped we'd keep returning to them so they could research Henry—put wires on him and test the synapses in his brain, follow the connections, the channels. To see how that thing between his ears worked.

But my mother wouldn't have it. Nope. He stayed right here, doing everything he was doing before, with joy and abandon. The only difference was that she did bring in this special instructor, on Saturdays, to "support, enrich, and participate" in all of his numerous obsessions.

Almost like a brain friend. Or a traveling companion to help Henry on his journey through his mind. To guide him, to instruct him, and to magnify him.

So, for instance, if Henry was building a robotic tree house, or a musical band of hamsters, or a ladybug chalet, the enrichment teacher would help him create *the most elaborate* robotic tree house, or ladybug chalet.

But that wasn't all. The tutor had a second task, tantamount to the first. To draw Henry, gently, into the world around him. Into the world of other people. To see them. To want to see them. To interact with them. To exist with them. On this plane. In this paradigm. In this world.

"Whatever *this world* is." (That's what my mom would always say. I'll get to that later. Kind of a doozy.)

The first order of business: to open Henry up to the world inside and outside his brain using the power of . . . magic.

Pick a card, any card. Silly tricks. Funny tricks. Terrible tricks. Tricks you'd never believe. And every week there would be a new box coming. A new kit. A new set of magic!

Dad thought there were too many boxes coming to the house but Mom thought the enthusiasm Henry showed justified the excess.

When Henry asked if he could give a magic show after dinner, we knew we had reached new territory. Suddenly after dinner wasn't just a time to sit back and hang loose or just do the dishes. Now after dinner was . . . the magic show. The magic show with rabbits. The magic show with doves. The magic show with a wand, a tablecloth, and a disappearing hamster.

And Dad never minded the boxes again.

But right now, under the night sky, with the waves crashing below, Henry, little Henry, has abandoned his magic. He is running straight down the slope, foot over foot, to the gate that leads to the stairs, to the sliver of beach . . . to investigate potential supernatural and/or scientific impossibilities.

I have a troubling thought as he crashes through the gate. What if I'm wrong? What if the presence I felt *is* dangerous? What if whatever that thing is down there is a trap?

Wait. What have I done?

"Henry! Heeeeen-ryyyyy! Stop! Wait!"

But he's not listening. Who knows if he can even hear me over the crashing of the waves? On stormy nights sometimes you can't even hear yourself for the tide battering the steep bedrock cliffs. It's worse than thunder.

And I don't know why this sudden dread has hit me, but I have to protect him. I have to make sure he doesn't catapult himself into the water, desperate to decipher the physics. I have to keep his tiny little bones intact in his tiny little body.

He's always been slight. Wiry. Just two big eyes on a stick of a body. Like a lollipop.

But he's barreling down the hill now and before I can stop him the gate is unlatched and banging in the wind, which means that he's probably halfway down the steps by now. The steep, serpentine steps, covered in the froth of the tide, slippery with moss, dangerous to even the most athletic, adult-type person.

"Henry! Wait! Wait uuuuuup!"

And when I get to the gate, clanking against itself, with the waves pummeling the rocks below . . . I look down. And I don't see him.

7

THIS IS THE moment I learn how to fly, rushing down the path and craggy bluffs through the salty sea air. Catapulting forward, possessed, and hurtling down down down, over the moss-covered rocks, down the steps, and into the cove. This is the moment I fall to the seashore, looking for Henry, and with him the last of the remnants of my heart.

And then—there it is again, that feeling I had just before. That thought that there was something in the air, some invisible thing, like longing, almost like the feeling just before rain. That feeling like something is just about to happen. When your body knows something your mind can't muster.

What it looks like, down there, and off the beach, the best way to describe it, is it looks like the northern lights. Blue and purple and even a little bit luminous. A light tornado. A whirling spectacle with a thousand twisting tendrils.

Whatever the thing is, it seems to be getting bigger, more energized, louder.

The whooshing sound is now thunderous.

FSHHHHHH. FSHHHHHH. FSHHHHHHHhhhhhhhh!

And beneath those screaming northern lights, on the beach hidden beneath the lone Torrey pine sticking out from the rocks—an impossible place to grow but it grows almost in defiance—is Henry.

Whew! Thank goodness.

He's writing something in the sand, with a stick, huddled over, deep in thought, just like when he's deep into one of his creations. He's writing something the way you'd take notes if your teacher is talking too fast. He's writing something desperate.

To see Henry after the thought—the thought I wouldn't let myself think—to see him after the idea that he, also, is taken away from me, means I have to catch my breath and thank God for a second. Call him the great creator, or the great programmer in the sky, whatever it is you want to believe. You *have* to believe it now that you've seen whatever *this* is whirling up in spires of blue and green and lilac, pirouetting up from the water, graceful and violent.

Henry looks up at me, sensing me over the rocks. He's cupping his ears, trying to decipher the horrible screech.

FSSSSSHHHHHHHHHhhhhh!

But just before I reach him, the enormous event, the gyrating lightshow thunder, comes to an immediate stop.

Poof.

Vanished. As if it were only meant for one.

Gone.

Henry and I stand there, in shock and awe, our knees about to give out beneath us.

8

AFTER A GOOD three minutes we start to collect ourselves.
Henry speaks first.

"Eva, did that . . . ? I know this sounds strange but did
that . . . seem like it was—"

"Trying to tell us something?" I finish his sentence.

My mother would say that's rude, but drastic times call for
drastic measures.

"Yes!" Henry goes on. "But how could that be? And what
was it trying to tell us?"

"I don't know. But it . . . that *thing* . . . it didn't seem dangerous. Did it?"

Henry shakes his head. "No. It didn't."

We stand there, befuddled, staring out past the breakers and across the sea.

"It didn't seem dangerous, but *how did we know that*?" He stands, still squinting at the sand.

"What do you think it means?"

We both look back over the deafening waves. "It defies logical explanation."

I smirk. "That's exactly what I was going to say. Except I was going to phrase it like 'That was so totally weird.'"

"There is, of course, the matter of this appearing-to-be-heretofore-unrecorded natural event."

Henry and I look at each other.

It's clear we have the same idea.

Dad used to put it like this: "When all else fails and you have no idea what is going on . . . research."

We used to roll our eyes every time he said this particular Dad-ism. But now I would kill to hear him say it.

Either way, we're following his advice.

It's time for research.

9

THE HOUSE IS much quieter now. The musings and laughter have died down and most of the guests have made their exit. There is only the sound of one surly, pickle-faced man, arguing to no one in particular.

There's always one of these. At every grown-up party. Without fail.

The first time my parents had to explain it to me, I was six. A friend of their friends, a German man from Frankfurt, had come to the party. When he first got to the party he was quite nice, actually. He even brought Henry and me a little wooden toy from Bavaria. This funny little paddle you would move left to right to make these colorful chickens move up and down, hand-painted in blue and red. We loved it, but my mom ended up putting it somewhere in a glass case, with the rest of her worldly curiosities.

However, the German man changed somewhere in the night. He went from being kind and reserved to something I had never seen before. He kept filling his glass and declaring things adamantly, pounding his fists on the table. Henry was already in bed by this point, with Marisol reading him a story. But Mom whisked me away, saying, "Time for bed, honey." I remember protesting—it wasn't time for bed. It was *way before* my bedtime. We hadn't even had dessert! But she was insistent.

On the way up the stairs, on the cherrywood landing, I remember saying to her, "Mom, what is going on with that guy?" She looked at me, not wanting to say. Not wanting me to know about this kind of thing yet. "Honey, do you mind if we talk about this in the morning? It's not that I don't think we should talk about it, because I think it's important and there's a lesson here. But . . . I'm kind of in damage control—"

And, as if on cue, a *CRASH* came from the dining room.

"—mode." My mother went rushing back in and I, of course, peeked in through the staircase. At first, it was hard to piece together what was happening. It was such chaos. But then, I realized, just as my mom realized, the German man had tried to stand up and had fallen backward into the glass case behind him. A tall glass case for her good china.

You know what I'm going to say next, right? Well you would be correct. The case, and the glass, and the china, all came crashing forward on top of the German man, where he lay now, muttering, covered in broken Willow ware and Wedgewood and shards of blown glass. The man, embarrassed and disoriented, began swearing in German, and the next thing you know, my dad and his colleagues were carrying him out, kicking and screaming in violent German. They put him in the car, still swearing, and someone volunteered to drive him home. It was an awful sight.

I remember rushing down the stairs to help my mother, or comfort her, or say bad things about the man, but she just smiled, scruffed my hair, and said, "Don't sweat it, kiddo. He's just really sick."

Sick?! I thought. How could he be sick? What was she even talking about? But she just picked up the Willow ware pieces and my dad came in to pick them up, too. Then he tried to send me back upstairs but, of course, I went rushing back to peer in when he wasn't looking. The forbidden fruit of adulthood shattered in pieces below the staircase. All the guests had cleared out and my dad and mom sat there, in silence. Then my mom said, "Well, at least he brought that toy."

They started laughing. The entire room looked like it had been struck by a hurricane but there they were, shaking their heads with the church giggles, chuckling. And I remember smiling, too.

It was always safe with them. Everything was always going to be okay.

10

WE'RE JUST OUTSIDE Dad's dark wood–paneled office, aka
Central Research Headquarters, when we hear her.

"And what, exactly, are you two kids doing up?"

It's Terri. It's not even the sound of her voice that gives it
away. It's that jingle of the ice in her glass. Like the jingle of
a bell on a storefront, there it is. An alert! Someone's coming.
Someone's here.

Henry and I turn to face her. She's leaning in the hallway
like the walls are the only thing keeping her up. She's got bright
red lipstick and long burgundy nails, and she's clutching that
glass to her chest like a baby bird.

"Aren't you little darlins' supposed to be in bed?"

"Yes, but—"

"Yesbut? That's not a word!"

"That doesn't even make sense," I respond. Henry is behind me, basically hiding. Whenever either Terri or Claude come around, Henry just sort of disappears. I do the talking.

"Oh, silly! It was just a joke. What's the matter? Don't you kids have a sense of humor?"

People always say that when they're not funny.

"No, it's just, we really just . . . we were looking for a book! Henry's favorite book! It's in here, so we wanted to get it so we could read it before—"

"Book, huh? What's it called?"

"You mean, the title?"

"Yes. The title of the book."

". . . *Brave New World*."

"Huh. Never heard of it."

Henry jumps in, suddenly excited.

"It posits a world not where people aren't allowed to read books, as George Orwell predicted in his novel *1984*, but a world where people wouldn't even *want* to read books, because they would be living in a state of 'infinite distraction,' medicating themselves with a happy pill, essentially. One could argue that his vision has essentially come to pass. That the infinite distraction of social media, the internet, and video games, in combination with the prevalence of antidepressants, is exactly, precisely, where we are now as a society."

Terri just looks at him.

"How old are you again?"

"Ten. He's ten." I nod. Henry disappears behind me again.

"Well, whatever. Time for bed. I can't be worrying about you kids up at all hours of the night. And I *do* worry about you, you know."

Um. Okay.

Henry's eyes cut to mine.

She leans down so her face is level with ours. "Now get on up to bed so I can turn in."

Henry and I look at each other, shrug, and head upstairs, reluctant.

I guess our research of the heretofore-unknown light-and-tornado phenomenon must wait.

Terri downs the rest of her drink and heads back downstairs, where the loud guest straggler is being ushered out, to muddled protests and continued very-important-points-he-must-make-right-this-second.

Henry whispers to me on the way up the stairs.

"Psst, Eva. Why do you think Terri just said she worries about us?"

"I have no idea. Maybe she needed a hug."

"I would rather give her a pug. Or possibly a slug."

"Like a slug like a snail with a house on its back? Or like a physical punch?"

"Definitely a snail," Henry says. "I'm a Buddhist. I do not believe in violence."

11

INSIDE OUR ROOM . . . my brother, who is apparently now a Buddhist, seems to be sinking back into himself after his brief return to the land of the living.

I'd love to ask him about his newfound appreciation of Eastern philosophy but, judging by the curve of his back, and his head hanging over the bed, this is not a good time.

"Henry?"

He just stays looking at the floor in silence.

Okay! Time to put on a show!

"You know, I wrote a little song, in honor of Terri the Terrible. Wanna hear it?"

A barely discernible nod. An opening.

"Okay, ready? One, two, three, four!"

Puff puff puff
Clink clink clink
All I do is smoke and drink.

I like to smo-oke.
I like to dri-ink.
A puff puff puff and a
Clink clink clink

I don't care what people think!
I just like to smoke and drink!

Henry stares at me, while I do a little box step with an invisible top hat and cane, ending with an imaginary hat tip, bow, and a flourish. There is a trace of a trace of a smile there.

I curtsy.

"Why do you think Terri smokes when it's clinically proven that smoking and exposure to secondhand smoke causes no less than four hundred and eighty thousand deaths a year?"

"That is a good question, Henry. I would say it's either because she doesn't care or because she's maybe not that smart or maybe some combination of the two."

"Perhaps I will tell her in the morning. Enlighten her."

"Somehow I think that might just make it worse. She seems to be on some sort of tear."

"Tear?"

"Yes, like she's angry at herself. For something."

"Hmm. Interesting hypothesis, my dear sister."

"I mean, doesn't it seem like it's getting worse? Her . . . peculiarity?"

"I have not made that observation. However, I have not been taking note."

"She's clearly upset about something. Do you mind if I ask you a question, Henry? What were you blanking out about, just then? Where did you go in that great brain of yours?"

"It's just . . . I felt something for a second. Down on the beach. Whatever that churning phenomenon was . . . there was a warmth to it. Something familiar. A kind of comfort. For a moment . . . it seemed like everything was fine again. As if nothing bad had ever happened."

He blinks at me, then puts his head on his pillow.

I know what that means. It means he doesn't want me to see him cry.

"Henry, we are going to be able to do this, you and me. It's going to be hard for a while. Maybe even terrible sometimes. But we have each other. We have each other and we just have to hold on together, hold each other up, you know?"

"What if I don't want to be held up? What if I just want to crash and burn?"

"Then hold me up, Henry. Because without you I feel like I'll just fall down straight into the center of the earth. Maybe even farther."

Henry looks up to me from his pillow. Eyes red from not-crying.

"I don't want that. Okay, Eva."

"Okay, Henry."

I stay with him a little while, until he falls asleep, Lego robot monster in hand. It's just about three in the morning when I creep into the bathroom to brush my teeth.

There's a mirror in there, framed by dark wood, surrounded by the mahogany-paneled room. The tile on the floor is little octagons, white with a little black diamond every once in a while. The light in there is a little bit funny. There is a yellowed sconce next to the mirror you have to turn off by hand.

All of that is normal, nothing strange. It's just . . .

I feel something again.

Something that's like a cousin—*related to* what I felt on the beach—but not quite the same. I look at the reflection of my arm in the mirror, and I can see the little hairs on it rise as if the temperature just dropped ten degrees.

I have the sense that there is something behind me. But I'm looking in the mirror, and there is nothing there.

I finish brushing.

I rinse and spit.

I reach up to the pull chain on the light.

It's just when I flick the light off, in the sconce there next to my reflection, that I see a distinct shape behind me, halfway down the hall.

I flip the light on again.

Nothing there.

I pull the chain and plunge the room back into darkness.

The silhouette. It's there again.

I turn around. "Ha!"

Nothing there.

No one at all.

Now each and every hair on my body is standing on end and I'm trying not to move, or breathe, or think. But if I was going to think, this is what I would think:

That was a man. A gray, skinny man in a hat, dressed in a funny little outfit that has nothing to do with our time.

And he was coming toward me.

12

MORNING.

No. I did not tell Henry I saw a terrifying figure in the hallway last night.

It's not that it slipped my mind, exactly. It's more in the ballpark of . . . well, he's got a lot on his plate. He doesn't need to wrestle with the idea that we are perhaps being stalked by a man-ghost from another time.

That's just not something you want to hear over breakfast.

Henry's making the waffle mix, Marisol is making the waffles, and I am adding a flourish of strawberries and whipped cream. It is to be noted that Henry's Blenderator 3000 is making the smoothies. What is a Blenderator 3000? Well, I'm glad you asked! Are you tired of cutting up all those messy fruits first thing in the morning? Do you ever wish you could just have that fresh fruit smoothie without all that backbreaking labor? Do you end up just eating doughnuts because you can't be bothered? Then you need the Blenderator 3000! It slices. It dices. It even puts the fruit in for you! Simple. Just put the fruit down, in front of the Blenderator 3000, sit back, relax, and watch it go!

(There is also a jingle I am working on.)

So the Blenderator is blending, and I am currently debating with myself whether to mention out loud the specter from the hallway of doom.

The three of us are sitting down to have our breakfast in the kitchen nook.

I decide to feel it out. "Um, Marisol? Have you ever . . . seen anyone in the house? Like maybe a weird old guy or something?"

"How many times do I have to tell you?! You can't leave the door unlocked, otherwise a bad man will come in and kill you with a knife!" Marisol warns.

"Or nunchuks." That is Henry's contribution.

"¡Sí! Nunchuks! Or any weapon, *realmente*. A club, a scissors, a stick!"

"A stick?" Henry isn't buying that.

"Okay, but I'm thinking more of a supernatural kind of thing," I add.

"¿*Un fantasma?* You mean like, how you say, a . . . a ghost?"

"Sort of," I reply.

"*Dios te salve, Maria, llena eres de gracia, el Señor es contigo . . .*"

Okay, so, Marisol is officially crossing herself and, I can tell by the little line in Henry's forehead, he is translating.

He mutters under his breath. "'Hail Mary . . . full of grace . . . the mister is with thee' . . . No! 'The Lord is with thee.' They call the Lord 'Señor.' Yes, that makes sense. He's essentially the preeminent mister. The biggest, best *señor*, so to speak."

"Okay! There's no reason to *pray*! I'm just asking . . . if you've ever noticed anything . . . funny in the house." I'm trying to calm everybody down but they are sort of both interpreting this new information in their own ways.

"Aye, Evita, there is nothing funny about a ghost! My *abuelita* used to have a ghost that would come and lick her in the night!"

Henry squints. "Are you sure that was a ghost?"

"Yes, we used to call him '*la lengua del más allá* . . . the tongue from beyond'!" Marisol makes a dramatic gesture, arms out.

"Um . . . I think we're getting really off-topic here. I just need to know if you've ever seen anything creepy around the house. At night. Upstairs."

As if on cue, there is Terri the Terrible in the doorway.

"I have," Marisol whispers, with a wink and a nod in Terri's direction. Terri doesn't hear.

"Why are you sitting down?" she accuses, looking at Marisol. "I'm sure you're not getting paid to sit around everywhere."

Henry stands up. "Marisol always sits with us at breakfast. She's part of our family."

"Oh, really? Is your name José?"

I stand in defiance. "Okay, that's really . . . *racist*. And if you were ever awake for breakfast you'd know that we eat with Marisol, like, every day. You're being, well, honestly, you're being horrible right now!"

Marisol begins clearing the dishes.

"See, that's right. Cleaning the dishes. That's called work. Nobody is hiring anyone to just sit around."

"OhmyGOD!"

I am on the verge of hyperventilating. So Henry attempts to explain. "Marisol is Guatemalan. From the Republic of Guatemala. The territory of modern Guatemala once formed the core of the Maya civilization—"

But Terri interrupts Henry.

"I don't care where she's from. Just because I'm not your mother doesn't mean I can be taken advantage of!"

"Okay, let's slow down here." I try to placate her. "Terri, I know that we may do things differently than you're used to, but Marisol has always been part of our family. And we need her now, more than ever. And right at this moment, we are eating breakfast. So if you have a problem with Marisol eating with us, then maybe *you should leave*."

Terri and I stare at each other. Everyone else in the kitchen is frozen. There is total silence.

This fine moment is interrupted by Claude the Clod clomping through the kitchen, grabbing a cup of coffee, barely noticing us, and clomping out.

Terri, as if following his cue, grabs her own mug and storms out.

Henry and I turn to Marisol.

"Marisol. I'm so sorry. We need you. Honestly, we do," I plead.

"It's okay, *mi vida*, there are always going to be people like that. Not everyone is like your parents. Or you."

There's a moment of silence now. All three of us missing the warmth and sanctuary of bygone days.

Marisol, trying to make it better, musses up Henry's hair and smiles.

"I'm going to the market today, but I'll be back, Henrito, and tonight we'll have your favorite paella. Don't worry, I will not leave the feet on this time."

She makes a claw gesture and a scary face, and retreats out the back of the house.

In case you're wondering, Marisol used to leave the chicken claws sticking out of the paella. It was a thing.

Henry and I continue eating our waffles.

"So, why were you asking about ghosts?" Henry wants to know. "Do you think it has something to do with that thing we saw last night?"

I shake my head. "It's nothing. I'm sorry I brought it up."

We chew our breakfasts. There's something like calm when—

Crrrrreeeeeeaaak.

The door to the pantry swings slowly open.

Henry and I look closer, craning our necks to see if someone is behind the door.

There's no one.

"Huh. Has that ever happened before?" Henry asks.

And then, as if to answer, the door slams shut.

WHAM!

It shakes in its frame and the two of us look at each other. Stunned.

Henry walks over to inspect the door. Opens it. Examines the hinges.

"Eva. If it weren't for the fact that I do not believe in paranormal activity, I would say this is paranormal activity."

"Yes, I don't believe in it, either, so obviously that didn't just happen."

"Right," Henry agrees. "Pass the syrup."

13

THERE MUST HAVE been a thousand little strange collectibles and tokens brought back to Henry and me by our mother. Every time she and Dad would have to go anywhere for work, she would come back with oodles of objects from the four corners of the globe. She would sit there, giddily watching as we opened our oddities. Dad would sit back, thinking it was just *too much*. But for Mom, it was never enough. She would tell him this way she was bringing us back the world. From the casbah of the Old City in East Jerusalem. From a tiny shop on stilts in Ko Samui. From a *tienda* near the Straits of Magellan.

It's just that she hated leaving us. This way, she would say, it felt like she wasn't really gone. Instead, she was just off running an errand for us.

She'd say she'd hear our little voices saying, "Yes, maybe this, and oh my God, what is that?!"

It makes it so much worse—knowing how much she hated leaving us.

I wonder if there are random gift shops in the sky? If there's a heavenly road paved with glittering cobblestones and there she is, looking around, picking up the various sparkling trinkets, my dad behind her, staring at his watch. But why would he be? There probably aren't watches up there. It's not like you need a watch in eternity. Or even time.

Suffice to say, if there are random gift shops in heaven, I'd put money on finding my mom there. I wonder if she's picking something out for me. Or Henry.

I wonder if she thinks she's still coming home.

Of all the things my mom ever brought Henry, this here was his favorite. This teepee. It's a ten-foot-high ivory-colored tent from the Standing Rock Sioux Reservation, and the outside is painted with burnt sienna and black, stripes near the bottom with triangles at the very top. In the middle, a scene of a hunt, warriors on horseback, twenty horses. At the top of the tent, wooden poles are fixed with leather straps at angles coming out, forming a kind of straw circle. It sits here, in the corner of our room, Henry's escape.

Inside, it is its own world. There are embroidered pillows in here, a buffalo-hide rug, and a tiny buckskin lamp. The light in here is a warm glow of amber. And now, the two of us sit here, squinting at his laptop, trying to solve the mystery of what we saw on the beach.

And what I saw in the hallway.

And what we saw in the kitchen.

Now that I think about it, perhaps we aren't just researching in here. Perhaps we are hiding.

"Giant tall whirlpool . . . ?" I offer.

Henry is curled over the keyboard, peering into the depths of the internet.

"Hydro spout? Definitely not. Ah, okay. Waterspout. Here we go." He sits up. "'Waterspout: A waterspout is an intense columnar vortex—usually appearing as a funnel-shaped cloud—that occurs over a body of water. Some are connected to a cumulus congestus cloud, some to a cumuliform cloud, and some to a cumulonimbus cloud. In the common form, it is a non-supercell tornado over water.'"

He looks over at me. I shrug.

"Would you categorize what we saw as a non-supercell tornado over water?"

I think about it. "I would categorize it as such . . . except in all these images the sky didn't look like the one we saw—with the colors and stuff."

Henry and I peruse the myriad of images for "waterspout." Most of the skies behind are bright blue. As if the waterspout appeared almost out of nowhere. Just waltzing along with the marble blue sky behind it. Like a happy, unexpected guest at a barbecue.

"Indeed," Henry agrees. "The sky we saw was a kind of purple gray . . ."

"Almost plum. Or the color of a bruise."

"Exactly. Also, let us not forget the acoustics."

"I would call what we heard a howling sound."

"But was it, exactly? It almost seemed like a distant voice—"

"—from another dimension? Maybe we should Google other dimensions."

Henry looks at me. "I'm fairly sure that will get us straight to UFO conspiracy-ville, complete with foil hats. Perhaps we should do a little more research on the ground, as they say."

"By *on the ground* . . . do you mean at the beach? Because I'm feeling pretty cozy in here, honestly."

"Yes. This is a comforting environment, but we are probably not going to uncover the answers we seek from the safety of this teepee. We must continue our research."

I yawn. "Well, if we just stayed here a little bit longer . . . I'm sure we could investigate further through the magic of the internet. Not to mention the low-level brain function you can access in your REM state, while you nap—"

But Henry is already out of the tent and filling his Minecraft backpack with investigative equipment. A magnifying glass. Microphone. Micro motion detector. Invisible ink pen.

"I'm pretty sure we won't need an invisible ink pen."

"Well, you never know. Also, it was part of the set."

I do have a vague recollection of Henry receiving this very spy set one Christmas.

"Wait. Didn't this come with binoculars? Also, we should have some sort of signal. A danger word. In case of emergency."

"Okay. The signal is: spaghetti," I suggest.

"Why spaghetti?"

"Well, it doesn't really seem like there would be any other excuse to use it."

"Okay, you're right. Spaghetti," Henry says, accepting this.

"Anyway, there's no reason to expect we'll be separated. We're just going down the hill."

We share a look. Even though there clearly *is* no reason we'd be separated, it's safe to say the last twenty-four hours have not exactly been by the book.

"You know, I just want to say again, Googling continues to be a valid option. You haven't even tried to search the term 'paranormal phenomena.' I mean, between the great bathroom ghost sighting and the infamous breakfast pantry door slamming, I think we have a lot to work with."

"Eva, we are not just sitting around here in the teepee. We are going to be bold. Remember what Dad used to say. 'Be bold, and mighty forces will come to your aid.'"

"I feel like mighty forces are definitely a part of this equation, but I'm not sure they are exactly coming to our aid."

Henry is already halfway down the hallway to the stairs.

I look around me. Suddenly, with no one else in the room, the possibility of paranormal sightings seems quadrupled.

"Wait! Hold on! I'm coming with you!"

14

THE TIDE IS pulled all the way out now, leaving a bed of slippery gray rocks, sand, and tide pools. Henry is ahead of me, inspecting the area below where the mysterious event originally took place.

I am leaning over the tide pools, studying a sea anemone with a microscope. This one is particularly lavender. One of Henry's many contraptions is clicking away as he holds a microphone out and over the seabed.

"Eva. Look at this. I am detecting some kind of electromagnetic interference."

He is literally holding a compass, a microphone, a digital recorder, and whatever that is making that repeated clicking noise. His head is tilted to one side, the microphone wedged between his chin and shoulder to keep it from slipping out into the breakers.

I love my brother. And he may be a boy genius, but he is no Ghostbuster.

I tell him, "I am detecting a sea anemone that has no right to be this bright a shade of purple."

He sighs. "Eva. Do you mind? Seriously?"

And he is right. I should be helping him. But something about this situation is making me nervous, and when I get nervous I tend to try to distract myself. With things I find comforting. Like sea anemones.

"Okay, okay. What am I looking for?"

"Just hold this microphone here while I try to detect the apex of the electromagnetic disturbance."

"Right."

Henry is slowly waving his outstretched arm in front of him. His pants are rolled up to his knees as he wades into the breakwater.

"Be careful, Henry. Those rocks are slippery. And there might be crabs!"

But Henry is definitely only hearing the gears inside his head as he waves the compass around in a steady semicircle, moving forward meticulously, collecting data.

To this point, most of this has just seemed to be an exercise in futility, but I begin to pick up something. A faint, if not imaginary, sound that could easily be nothing more than the wind through the eucalyptus trees.

Henry must hear it, too, because he turns. "What is that?"

I shrug, holding out the equipment, not wanting to speak over the sound.

"Are you sure you're recording?" he asks.

"Yes! I think."

He looks back at me and rolls his eyes.

We stay still, trying to pick up the elusive whistling noise. It seems to come to a kind of crescendo and then falls away, fading into the sound of the surf over the rocks.

"Do you think we got it?" he asks.

"Who knows. I don't even know what *it* is."

"Well, stay there while I clear the area. Best to collect as much data as possible." He continues forward, the bottoms of his rolled-up pants soaked past his knees.

I watch as he begins to move out, wading farther and farther into the water, moving millimeter by millimeter. I have a feeling this is going to take a while.

"Can I sit? I can still record if I'm sitting, you know."

"No sitting. Just stay there," he answers.

Now it's my turn to roll my eyes.

This goes on for about a billion years.

Finally, after Henry has pretty much combed the entirety of the shore, he comes back, flushed and a little bit sunburned.

"I forgot to put on sunscreen. Mom would kill me."

There's a moment here—just a split second—when we both remember a time when our biggest worry was sunscreen.

"Okay. I've determined the center of the disturbance, if that can even be calculated by the electromagnetic discrepancies, which is my current hypothesis."

I nod. "Of course."

(*Entre nous*, I have no idea what he's talking about.)

"Right there. You see that rock there? The one that kind of looks like a leaning pyramid? Two rocks over from that. There. That's the center."

"Okay. Great." I look at him. "So, now what?"

"I think if we play back the recording, digitally analyzing the sound . . . we might be able to triangulate each phenomenon and ascertain if there is some correlation between the audio and the electromagnetic center of the abnormality."

"The pheno-electro who?"

"We can see if the clicks and the noise from yesterday are related."

"Great. And then what?"

"And then . . . I don't know exactly."

The sun is starting to dip down into the sea, turning the clouds out west a shade of rose gold. We both look out over the lavender-painted sky.

Henry says, "I'd like to stay here a while, if you don't mind."

This is an unusual request from my kid brother. In fact, I can't remember Henry ever asking to just sit down and do nothing. Watching the sun set over the Pacific Ocean, this was always more of a Dad request. He was always the one trying to get us to stop and smell the roses or whatever.

I nod to Henry and we walk up just below the stairs, sit

down on two flat rocks, and take in the vista. The sky is painting everything into an orange-and-pink blaze.

There is too much to think about. Between the super-strange waterspout, the mysterious sound over the waves, the bathroom ghost sighting, and the lone kitchen pantry door slamming, I'm actually starting to wonder if we might be going a little bit crazy. I mean, it is a distinct possibility. We have been through a terrible trauma. What if, as a result, we are both just simultaneously losing our minds?

"Do you think we imagined it? The pantry door this morning?"

"Maybe," he answers.

"What about the thing I thought I saw during the execution of my routine dental hygiene?"

"Quite possibly."

"And maybe the waterspout?"

"Eva, there is the possibility all of these are natural-occurring phenomena that we have imbued with some sort of otherworldly meaning due to psychological stressors. In fact, that is probably the most logical explanation."

Something Dad used to say swims up to the surface of my brain. "Occam's razor . . ."

Henry nods. "Among competing hypotheses, the one with the fewest assumptions—the simplest answer, in other words—should be selected."

"Right. So everything could be normal. Like *totally* normal. Except us."

"Yup."

I put my arm around Henry's shoulder. We stare out over the breaking waves. The sun is cut in half now, a gold semicircle above the horizon with the rest disappeared over the edge of the earth.

"I'm going to choose that answer," I decide. "The one where we are just imagining things. Akmed's razor."

"Occam's."

"Right."

Henry thinks. "I will, too. And if we're crazy, well, at least we're crazy together."

This is my favorite millisecond . . . that tiny moment when the sun hides itself behind the horizon and the only thing left is a little sliver . . . and then a tiny spot. Just a dot on the horizon of blazing light. Like everything in the world is contained, concentrated in that one shiny speck at the edge of everything you know.

And I can choose to believe that everything is normal. That the sky is blue and water is wet and that, no matter what, the sun always rises in the east and forever will set in the west.

Except for the very next thing that happens.

The one that proves we are definitely *not* crazy.

15

IT'S ALREADY DARK by the time we make it up the hill, neither of us wanting to go back to the realm of Terri the Terrible until the last second. The trees reach up to the sky, black silhouette arms spindling up to the stars, each turning on one by one.

If we wanted to, we could have been full of fear. If we hadn't decided everything was normal. Which we definitely had.

We decided! Totally normal.

So normal, in fact, that I believe a song is in order.

Something chipper.

Everything is swell.
Everything is fine.

No need to feel
It's out of line.

It's all just perfect.
It's all just swell.
Don't you worry now.
All will be well.

"Eva."

"No, don't stop me, I'm figuring out the chorus."

"Evaaa."

"I'm thinking maybe a key change here and—"

"EVAAAAAA!"

"Jeez, what the heck?" I pause my magnum opus, facing Henry.

He does look a little . . . pale.

"Turn around."

"What?"

"Just—*turn around* . . ."

Something in Henry's voice tells me I most definitely should *not* turn around because there is obviously something hideous, something terrifying, something too ghastly to be seen somewhere behind me.

"M-M-Maybe I won't?" I stutter.

"I think you should."

I squint at him, *avec* purpose, sizing him up. Maybe he's just playing a trick on me. Maybe this is just some bit of psychology, like trying to scare someone when they have the hiccups.

"Okay, I'm not falling for it."

"Fine. Don't turn around. It's getting closer anyway."

It?

Is getting *closer* . . . ?

It is at this terrifying moment that I turn around. I can honestly tell you, ladies and gentlemen of the jury, if there were any sight that I could randomly bestow on another human being, it would *not* be this one.

I never, neither in a million years nor for a million dollars, would randomly bestow this sight on even my very worst enemy.

Because what I'm facing—is an army of incorporeal souls.

Los fantasmas.

Ghosts.

And they? Are shambling toward me.

16

THERE WAS ONCE a time when we were little. A festive time when we went over to our dad's work colleague's house for a holiday party. It was a random, one-off thing and we never went back, partly because my mom was extremely annoyed at the extent to which the parents let their children play Minecraft. Not only was there screen time, but there was *no limit* on screen time. So, basically, all the kids at the party were just shuffled aside into the basement (dungeon) and put in front of a bunch of tiny screens to drool all over themselves the whole night and probably damage their eyes permanently.

I still remember my mother on the way home. Henry was already asleep in the back seat and I was supposed to be asleep but I couldn't help relishing this little moment of unfiltered adult-talk eavesdropping.

"I mean, if I had known, I would have brought Marisol. At least that way they could have played, or made up a puppet show, or done some crafts—" Mom lamented from the passenger seat.

"I know, honey. But you know, different strokes for different folks. I'm sure one night won't damage the kids for life."

This is my dad, always true blue, always seeing the other side.

"I get it, but it's just the principle of the thing. And those kids?! Do they just park them in front of the screen all day? That one game had guns in it! Machine guns! And everybody blowing everybody up. He couldn't have been more than five!"

"That is pretty extreme," Dad allowed. "I wonder if they knew he was playing it?"

"I mean, what kind of a society are you making when you put machine gun video games in front of five-year-olds? It's no wonder we're caught up in endless wars!"

From the back seat I remember my dad, looking over at my mom, putting his hand on her hand. God, he loved her. If every husband loved every wife like that? I don't think we'd even have wars.

But the thing I remember most from that party is the moment one of the big kids decided to play an R-rated movie on his iPad. All of us kids, there were about twenty of us, circled around to watch the inappropriate, not-for-our-consumption movie.

Henry was the only kid who wasn't watching, and that's

because he was conducting an experiment with cleaning supplies.

I remember wanting to be brave, wanting to be a big kid, and wanting to show I could watch the super-scary movie, too.

It was only the part when the zombies came out of the ground and started coming forward in droves, trying to eat brains, that any bravery I might have mustered up decided to hightail it out of my body.

The good news is, Henry mixed ammonia with baking soda and accidentally exploded an entire Costco bulk package of paper towels. The bad news is, that kind of ended the party.

Now that I think of it, I'm sure for all the lamenting my mom did on the drive home, the hosts of that party were probably dragging our parents' names through the mud for letting their kid conduct dangerous science experiments in the basement unsupervised.

So, you see, it all comes out in the wash.

You're probably wondering why I'm telling you this.

Welp, that would be because, um, those zombies coming out of the ground in the R-rated movie and scaring the tuna salad out of me all those years ago at the Christmas party? Yes, those selfsame zombies were across the lawn, coming toward us from the hill sloping down to the east, which also happens to be the location of the *family cemetery*.

Gulp.

17

"DON'T MOVE."

"Uh . . ."

I am currently frozen in fear. So Henry telling me not to move is a bit redundant.

Allow me to describe the macabre vista before me. The lawn, usually green but now purple underneath the starlight, spreads down from where we are, the path from the cliffs, all the way to the other side, where the centuries-old ancestral cemetery is tucked away behind a giant magnolia tree. In front of us, too far away, is the house. Behind us is the cliff, which is about a fifty-to-sixty-foot drop-off to the water below.

So, you see, unless we want to become zombies and eat brains for the rest of our undead unlives, we better think fast.

"Are those . . . zombies?" I manage to utter in despair.

"They can't be zombies. There's no such thing as zombies."

"They sure look like zombies."

"That's not logical. There's no such thing," Henry tells himself.

The good news is, whatever they are, they're moving slowly. I'd say at about the pace of an octogenarian carrying a giant bag of groceries. In front of you. At the grocery store. So . . . *so* slow it's almost unfathomable.

As they inch their way closer, I begin to make out their clothing. As does Henry.

"Interesting. Their clothes appear to be early nineteenth, maybe eighteenth century. Definitely Victorian era. And they don't seem decomposed in the way of traditional zombies." He thinks for a moment, then snaps his fingers. "Aha! I've got it. They're not zombies."

"Okaaay."

"Perhaps the electromagnetic field has allowed for some kind of paranormal transmittance," Henry postulates.

"In English."

"Those are definitely ghosts."

"Right."

The ghoulish figures are about fifty feet away from us now, which is fifty feet too close, wobbling toward us like molasses. I count five of them.

"One . . . two . . . three . . . four . . . five. Do you see any others, Eva?"

I can't help it. I shriek, *"Is this actually happening right now?"*

As they approach, their skin begins to reveal itself. Cloudy, translucent skin, seemingly wavering in and out of this plane of existence. In one second, they are there, you could swear it. The next, they seem like nothing more than a wave, or even the thought of a wave.

". . . But why aren't they speaking?" Henry whispers, more to himself.

"Maybe they don't talk." I shrug.

"So they are silent ghosts?"

"Maybe they don't want to be rude. Like they don't want to yell. Or cause a disturbance." I'm just making stuff up now.

"Do you think they're here to harm us?"

"I don't know, why don't we stand here frozen and ask them while they devour our souls and usher us down to the netherworld?" I suggest.

"According to my calculations, we could stand here another five minutes and easily make it to the house, with time to spare."

And this is true. During that entire exchange, they have only advanced about five feet.

Henry nods. "I'm going to go see what they want."

I grab his arm. "Wait! What?! What are you talking about?"

"It falls to reason that if they wanted to hurt us, we'd be dead already. Quite frankly, they are supernatural beings. With powers of which we can't possibly conceive!"

"I have an idea," I say. "Why don't we just shoot video of them. We can post it on YouTube. Then all the ghosts scientists—"

"Parapsychologists."

"Then all the para-whatever-itses will see it and figure it out and we can just stay in our beds."

"I understand your theory, Eva, and your trepidation. However, they might not be visible to other carbon-based life-forms."

"Excuse me?"

"It's possible only we can see them." Henry dumbs it down.

"Why would you think that?"

The ghost menagerie is now forty feet away from us.

"Listen, Eva. Has anyone else mentioned any paranormal activity in the house? Marisol? Claude? Terri? No. No one has."

"Maybe the bathroom ghost of dental hygiene just wasn't interested in them," I contend. "Maybe the ghost is just concentrating on *our* dental habits because we're younger and therefore more impressionable and they just want to make sure we have a positive relationship with flossing and our teeth in general. Including gum health. Which is very important."

But Henry is still analyzing the battalion of ghosts before us, indifferent to my supernatural dental health hypothesis.

"What could they possibly want from us? They're clearly disinterested in the house. Their focus seems to be on you and me."

"Right. Which makes me think our focus should be on getting the heck out of here," I offer.

"Aren't you curious?" Henry asks.

"I'm curious in the way someone would be curious if a

knife-wielding bandit approached them and asked for their lunch money. Like, there would be questions about who that person was, why they were wielding a knife, and why such overkill just for lunch money. But . . . I wouldn't want to stick around to find out the answers."

"Your feelings are registered." He nods.

"Great. So, let's go."

"KIDS!" The yell comes from the other direction. "Kids, what in the world are you doing out here? It's freezing! Your uncle has been worried sick!"

Henry and I both turn to see Terri running out in slipper-heels and an overcoat. Even though she didn't have time to put on actual shoes, she did not forget to bring her cocktail.

"Wait." Henry stops me. "Look. Terri doesn't seem to see them."

And indeed. Terri seems to be running toward us with abandon, not a care in the world, other than the wind batting her sideways and the liquid even in her drink.

"Her trajectory will directly bisect the ghosts if she keeps on her current vector— Oh my!"

Henry stops his science class short.

"What?"

"They're gone."

I turn to the coterie of ghosts and yes, indeedy-doo, they are completely vanished, disappeared, *fin*.

"What the—?"

"Don't say anything," he mutters.

"You mean, like, *Hey did you just see that armada of zombies on the lawn?*"

"Exactly."

"Kids, dinner is ready! If you don't come in right now I swear to God—"

"We're coming, we're coming!" we shout back.

Henry and I share a look.

Well, this is awkward.

No, there's nothing strange about rejoining our family inside after sharing a supernatural encounter on the lawn with five geriatric ghosts. This is all totally by the book. Cake.

Nothing to see here.

Nope, nothing at all.

18

DESPITE THE GREAT paranormal encounter Henry and I have just experienced, the two of us are sitting calmly, even intently, at the dinner table. Terri is regaling us with tales of her many days as a lasso star in the rodeo.

I know, I know. I was surprised to hear it, too.

But it just goes to show you, never judge a smoking, drinking, shopping, and phone-addicted book by its cover.

"You know, I kinda miss that old show . . . kitschy thing that it was," Terri waxes on. "Of course, that was long before I met your uncle."

This room is extremely dark, with deep walnut wood paneling halfway up the walls where it abruptly turns to burgundy damask wallpaper. There are sconces on the walls, yellowed by decades of use. A crystal pendant chandelier twinkles down from the ceiling in a million winking sparkles. Terri looks up into it, as if looking into a crystal ball.

"You should have seen it. Waco had never witnessed anything like it, before or since! Three lassos, all at once!" Then Terri shakes her head, beaming. "Now that was a great day."

"Maybe you should take it up again. The lasso? Lassoing. Whatever you're supposed to call it," I suggest.

She looks at me, lost for a second, as if my voice is dragging her back from the dusty plains and miraculous days of the Texas Panhandle.

"What? Oh, shoot. That's ancient history." She brushes it off, glances at Claude, and finishes in a near whisper, "I have a different life now."

True, but I can feel a part of her still there. Lasso in hand.

Hmm. I would not have guessed somewhere beneath all that face paint was a real live Calamity Kate. I guess you really never know about folks until you start asking questions.

I vow to ask more questions.

My dad used to love to say, "Never judge a man until you walk a mile in his shoes. That way you're a mile away and you have his shoes."

Claude has been texting this whole time, grumbling to himself.

"Honey, are you planning on eating anything?" Terri nudges him.

"What? Oh. Yes, it's just . . ."

And then he goes back to texting.

Whatever real estate deal it is Claude is working on, it does *not* seem to be going well. Every so often he stress-shovels some food in his mouth and keeps texting.

His annoyance is palpable.

Henry and I look to Terri. She shrugs and then takes out her own phone.

"Well, this has all been very enlightening, but perhaps it's time to retire," Henry suggests, nodding to me.

"Oh, uh, yeah. I'm pretty tired. Truly a wonderful meal. Thanks, Marisol!"

But Marisol is in the other room, binge-watching *Planet Earth*. She should be sitting here with us, of course, but first there is Terri, and second that episode she's watching, with the lizards and snakes, is practically *Star Wars* with reptiles. Totally engrossing.

We make our way to the stairs. This entire staircase area from top to bottom is covered in books, serving as a kind of library nook in the middle of the house. There's even a little settee with a reading lamp at the bottom, in case anyone decides to just sit down and get themselves lost in a story in the middle of the stairwell.

Of course, there is the possibility that Henry and I are a bit nervous about shuffling up said stairs by ourselves, given the recent uptick in paranormal experiences.

We both halt immediately at the bottom.

"Wait. Why did you stop?" Henry asks.

"Why did *you* stop?" I reply.

"Clearly, I stopped because you stopped."

"No, you stopped first."

"Well, honestly, what does it matter?"

"Maybe it matters because it's weird we just both stopped randomly—and simultaneously."

"I see. You think there's something intangible, imperceptible, only discernible by our subconscious stopping us."

Somehow that sentence terrifies me.

Henry and I share a look.

And then, at the exact same moment, we both tear up the staircase with all our might, various elbows and knees flying as we bound up two steps at a time, up up up the stairs and toward our room.

Wouldn't it be great if all of this actually *was* our imagination? If there was absolutely no explanation for why Henry and I seemed to have sensed something there at the bottom of the stairs?

Well, I'm sorry to disappoint you, but that is not the case.

Because we're nearly to the second floor when something very strange happens. At first it's just one book, then two, then three, then four, then five, six, seven, eight, nine, fifty, one hundred, then *all* the books begin flying out from their shelves—flying out and circling around in the midstair landing—swirling higher and higher like some scholarly tornado, up up up, creating a kind of . . . literary hurricane. It occurs to me that this sight is not unlike the one we experienced on the shore, with the water and the lights and the strange feeling of *un*dangerousness. But I have no time to say any of that, as we are too busy escaping the wrath of the library tornado, ending up safe and sound, quiet and calm, back in our bedroom.

And that's when we see it.

Or rather them.

The five ghosts from the cemetery.

They're here. And they seem to have made themselves at home.

19

IT IS A fine tableau gathered in front of the far wall of our bedroom. Five spiritual beings are standing, sitting, leaning, and even lounging, all with their eyes trained directly on us.

I open my mouth and fill my lungs with air. I am about to scream when—

"Well, thank goodness! We thought you'd never arrive!"

This comes out of the transparent mouth of a rather pale, plump female figure. Said figure is wearing an ornate tiara and a bejeweled ball gown, and holding a rather large, elaborate feather fan.

Henry and I turn to each other.

"Pinch me," Henry asks.

"What? Why?"

"Eva, please. Just pinch me."

"Fine." I pinch him extra hard.

"Ow!" Henry rubs his arm. Then he stares across the room. "Still there."

"Now, now, kids, quit it! We don't have time to lollygag around! Time's a-wasting!"

At this, Henry and I turn to what can only be described as a dusty, gritty, suspendered yokel in knee-high boots, wearing a broad hat, holding a gold mining pan.

"Howdy! Name's Beaumont! Beaumont Eugene Billings. But you can call me Beau. Heck, you're kin. Blood kin, at that!"

"Blood . . . kin . . . ?" The words sound themselves out in Henry's mouth, not sure where they're supposed to be.

"Darn tootin'! Why, who do you think built this house? And with what gold? Me, that's who! Don't be scared. Just because I glow a little does not mean I bite."

And now I recognize him. This is the bathroom ghost. The one I saw in the mirror behind me the other night. I'd swear my teeth on it.

"Wait a minute. I know you—"

"You know all of us, darling. Or you should," the woman in the long dress declares. "This is your great-great-great-*great*-grandfather, Beaumont Eugene Billings. The gold miner. And I'm his wife, Plum. And these two, over here"—she gestures to two extremely sophisticated gentlemen, in tuxedos and top hats, both of them sipping martinis with their noses high in the air—"are our sons, August and Sturdevant."

"Quite, quite." They nod, raising their glasses in an imaginary toast. As they drink, the liquid basically just pours through them, onto the floorboards.

"And this here's my granddaughter, Maxine. Don't mind her, she's depressed."

She gestures to the 1920s flapper, languidly lounging in the corner in a thousand-tassled dress, like someone straight out of *The Great Gatsby*. She wears a jeweled headdress around her short, black, bobbed hair, and holds out a long, lean cigarette holder. The smoke rises up, through her translucent body, to the rafters above.

"Why shouldn't I be depressed? We're dead, after all." Her voice is like a droll lullaby.

"Oh, dagnabbit! What did I make all this money for if my brood is just gonna sit around like a bunch of ninnies!" the gold miner, Beau, exclaims. "Buck up, children, we have work to do!"

Plum rolls her eyes, then returns her gaze to us. "Don't worry, kids. We are here for a reason, one other than to bicker like schoolchildren." She pauses. "No offense."

"None taken," Henry mutters. The two of us stand there, still trying to convince ourselves this isn't a dream.

"Henry? Is this really happening?" I whisper under my breath. "Are there ghosts here . . . speaking to us?"

But before he can answer, Plum begins.

"Beaumont, my love, come on now. Explain."

The plump ghost nods to Beaumont, who now also happens

to be smoking a corncob pipe. The billowing smoke fills up his transparent body and then goes directly through him, up to the ceiling. There sure is a lot of smoking going on around here. Times have changed.

"Heck. Why me, Plum?"

"Because you've always had a knack for explaining things. You're a storyteller. That's what the townsfolk used to say." She turns to us. "A real whippersnapper!"

As if on cue, Beaumont and his corncob pipe step forward in all their dusty glory.

"What my dear wife, Plum, is trying to tell you is that we here are your relatives. Your ancestors, if you will. There is not a being in this room with whom you, you little scamps, do not share blood."

"Get to the good part!" Plum elbows him.

"Goshdarnit, lady. Gimme a chance!" Now Beaumont turns back to us. "As you can see, we are not here to harm you, although our spectral figures may seem to spell peril, diabolic intrigue, or even doom. Do not be afraaaaaaid!"

He seems to relish this.

"Quite right, quite right," August and Sturdevant concur.

Beaumont continues, "For we are here for one purpose, and one purpose only. To seek justice! More specifically, to seek justice for our kin. You see, it has come to our eternal attention that our great-great-great-grandson, one William Alexander Billings, and his lovely wife, Margo, have been the victims of foul play."

Henry and I stand motionless. We blink once. Twice.

"As these are your most beloved parents and as you are our kin as well, it naturally falls to us to right this great wrong. That is why we are so passionate about the issue at hand! A-CHOO!"

He sneezes. Somehow this sneeze leads to an even louder sneeze.

"Aaaa-CHOOO!"

"*Gesundheit*," Plum blesses him.

"Excuse me, urchins! My lungs never could stand this damp climate! Give me the Great Plains back in Nebraska, I say!" Beaumont says.

"This is not happening," I say out loud.

"Quit getting sidetracked, Beaumont!" This interruption comes from Plum, who snaps her feathered fan.

"Okay, like I said. We—me, August, Sturdevant, Maxine, and of course, my wife, Plum here, who has clearly deemed herself the communications expert—"

Plum chuckles.

"—we've come to represent the family," Beaumont continues. "The Billingses! What do we seek, say you? Justice. Justice for our beloved kin, your dearly departed parents."

"Wait. What are you saying, even? If you exist at all? Which, honestly, right now . . . I'm not sure," I burst out. Henry nudges me.

Plum steps forward. "Dear children, what my articulate husband here is trying to tell you is that the death of your mother and father . . . it was no accident on the sea. No, no."

"I'M NOT SURE I understand," Henry says. "If what you say is true . . . why aren't our parents, or *their spirits*, here? Why can't they tell us? Rather than you? No offense."

"Isn't it obvious?" Maxine muses from the back.

"Look, kiddos. Ghosting ain't easy. In fact, it takes years, even decades, to master it. Why, it took me half a century!" Beaumont proclaims.

"Quite right, quite right." The top hats nod.

"And what you're seeing here, well, kids, this is the best we could do. It's all we've got. No one else was yet up to the task! And we've been ghosts for a *long* time," Plum admits. "For our first haunting, we did pretty well, wouldn't you say? I mean, we certainly got your attention."

Plum looks around and the ghosts nod.

"Must be hard to believe you've got so much kin in one room. Looking out for you." She smiles kindly.

And it is true. In this ridiculous room, surrounded by these five individual ghosts, there's a feeling I never would have expected to find, in all my life.

Love.

"I don't understand. The supernatural activity. The readings on my electromagnet-o-meter—" Henry is trying to piece it together. "That was . . . you?"

Plum shakes her head. "Nooooooo . . . it was some of our . . ." She searches for the right words. "Newer members?"

Henry gasps. Tears brim and threaten to spill out of his eyes.

"I don't get it," I tell him.

"See, that's what we're telling ya kids. Ghosting ain't easy!" Beaumont adds.

Wham! Someone might just as well have punched me in the gut. I get it now. Or I think I do. "Wait, so that thing . . . on the beach . . . that was—it w-w-was . . ." I'm stuttering now.

Beaumont nods his head. "Trying to get through. It ain't easy. No, sir."

Henry and I are clasping each other's hands for dear life.

The room spins. Dizzy.

"So . . . they. Our parents? They . . . can see us?"

"Oh, yeah. Heck, yeah!"

"Beaumont! No need to swear in front of the little ones!" Plum corrects him.

"Yep, kiddos. They can see you. Sure as you can see us. They just can't get to you. Not yet, anyway. Why do you think they sent us?" Beaumont asks.

"Even I admit it's quite moving," Maxine purrs from the corner.

"Indeed, indeed," August and Sturdevant chime in.

"Lookit, we're running out of time now," Plum interjects. "We'll be back just as soon as we can, but, in the meantime, you know what to do."

Henry and I nod.

"Wait. What? What do we do?"

Plum, Beaumont, Maxine, August, and Sturdevant all look at each other. A moment of concurrence. Maxine gets up from her languid chaise lounge and floats over, right in front of us.

"Why, darlings. You must *avenge their death*."

And with that, as if the last word was a charm, the lights dim down and the translucent figures seem to go with them, flickering in and out, down, down, fading into the darkness, finally . . . into the pitch black.

I know Henry is standing next to me, still as a statue. Just as I know that when we turn on the light the room will once again be empty. But whether this is a charm, or a curse, or a dream, or even something I'm making up to save myself from blind despair—whether this is a last gasp before madness—I don't know.

What I do know is that I now live in a world where ghosts? Are an actual thing.

PART TWO

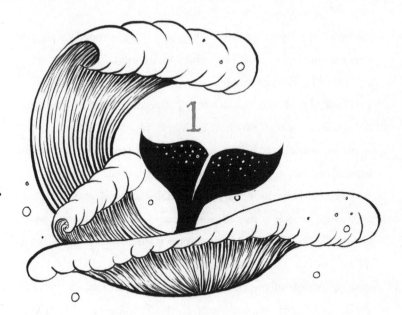

LIFT THE LEVER and that's how you open the attic. The lever looks like a decorative Mesopotamian fertility figure on the wall, so it's a little bit strange. But all you have to do is turn it slightly to the right and the trapdoor to the attic opens. You have to jump out of the way, though, because the stairs come immediately falling down from above and, as I learned the first time around, can bonk you on the head.

Most people do not go into their attic. Or, if they do, it's to collect a few antiques, photographs, knickknacks, old clothes, or yearbooks boxed up somewhere in the nether between stuff to be kept in the house, stuff to give away, stuff to throw away, and stuff nobody can even begin to figure out what to do with.

There is usually an old dusty rug rolled up somewhere in the corner, maybe a collection of baseball cards, and, always, a greater collection of spiders.

However, that is not what is happening here in this attic. No, indeed. Not in this house. When he was five, Henry took it upon himself to begin building his robot laboratory right here above our very own home. And, yes, there are robots. Little ones. Mostly the kind you can drive around with a remote control. There are, in addition, potions. Science experiments. Goop. Goop with electrodes. Goop with connecting currents. Three ant farms. Two snail hotels. One ladybug chalet. A rather vast collection of multicolor beetles, each encased in glass; an entire Lego universe consisting of the Spookyville, Ninjaland, and Minecraft worlds, and the Strawberry kingdom, which is the medieval section, ruled by Lightning Bolt, the king, and his second-in-command, Peter PotatoChip. There is, also, an entire corner dominated by a magnet experiment where Henry is trying to learn how to levitate objects of different weights with a varying magnetic current. So, as you can see, it's pretty busy.

Right now, Henry and I are secretly up here in the dark, under the pretense we are actually in our beds sleeping, to have an extremely important debate over what we just experienced.

"It's statistically impossible that we would both hallucinate the exact same thing, verbatim, both visually and physically," Henry contends.

"Totally. Also, did that really happen?!"

"It's easy enough to check the records, to account for the ancestral relations."

"I'm pretty sure I remember Dad talking about a relative from Iowa, who came to California with only a dream of mining for gold. Clearly, that must be Beaumont, his great-great-great-grandfather, who discovered gold during the 1849 Gold Rush and then built this house in the first place. You know, forty-niners and all that," I recall.

Henry nods. "They're a funny little lot, aren't they?"

I smile back. "Yeah, I kind of like them. Especially Maxine. She's glamorous in that flapper dress with all those silver tassels everywhere."

Henry and I stay silent for a moment, not wanting to say what we both are thinking.

"So, do you think they're right?" I ask.

Henry hesitates and looks at his Lego kingdom. A blue Lego knight on a white horse is positioned, just about to charge the castle with a joust.

"Quite frankly, I don't know what to think."

I nod. "But, seriously. *Foul play?* I mean, shouldn't we at least investigate just to be sure?"

Henry contemplates, his gaze still fixed on the little Lego knight.

"Absolutely. We should investigate. In an unbiased and rational manner. Then, we should proceed with caution, weighing the evidence. Logically."

"You're right. We should keep our emotions out of it." I

nod. Even though that's impossible.

"I believe we have to start somewhere. Let's listen to the audio, shall we?"

"Audio?"

Henry is immediately bounding around the attic, gathering items from our foray out to the beach, presumably to investigate the great waterspout incident. He's muttering to himself, which means the wheels are acutely in motion.

"Backpack. *Check.* Electromagnet-o-meter. *Check.* Audio. *Check.* Digital enhancer. *Check.* Audio editor. *Check.* Audio diffuser. *Check.*"

He is his own kind of whirling dervish now, zigging and zagging about the attic, collecting and connecting, scratching his head, reconfiguring and scratching again. There are a few zaps, zips, and even a little periodic smoke coming out of what can only be described as his command center over there in the corner, underneath the looming marble run.

"Okay, so, Henry. What exactly are you doing?"

"I, my dear sister, am digitally enhancing the mysterious sound from the sea in the general area of the waterspout and electromagnetic field. Remember? That *scree* of a sound we heard over the waves?"

I nod. "Do you really think you're going to find anything?"

He shrugs. "At least if it's nothing we'll know it's nothing."

As I watch Henry peering into the myriad switches, gears, wires, sensors, and lights of his home-fangled audio center, I can't help but feel a moment of big-sisterly pride that of all the kid brothers in the world I happen to have the only one who may not be able to have a conversation featuring sports, reality shows, or poop humor, but can single-handedly create a DIY electronic analysis center to rival the equipment at the lab of probably the most advanced third-world country.

WELP, SOMEWHERE IN the middle of all the buzzing and whirring, Henry and I both fell asleep. I don't blame us. We did start all this around midnight.

I'm currently having a dream about diving off the Eiffel Tower into the magical Parisian evening, complete with a stray accordion in the distance. I fly peacefully, gliding over the gargoyles of Notre Dame, the steps of Montmartre, and even through the arch of the Arc de Triomphe down the Champs-Élysées when the sound of a beautiful woman sings to me:

"Evaaaa. ¡Evitaaa! Cielito lindoooo . . ."

Now the singing turns to calling and I look up to see Marisol. Her straight black hair cascading down her shoulders in the dusty light.

She's poking her head through the attic trapdoor and, in my bleary, confused eyesight, looks just like two giant eyes with spiders for eyelashes.

"*¡Ay, mi vida!* Why you up here in this creepy place with all these spiders, you are supposed to be sleeping in your clean little beds like two little angels and not here like stowaways on *La Bestia!*"

Henry wakes up, rubbing his eyes. *"¡Buenos días, Marisol! ¿Cómo estás, hoy?"*

"I am fine except for the fact that my two little precious angels are asleep on this dusty floor in the attic like *vagabundos*. I didn't find you in your beds and I started breathing in and out, in and out, like running a marathon. You better not give me gray hairs or I will never forgive you!"

But she is smiling, relieved she found us, and there's nothing Marisol can say that wouldn't come out to us like warm honey on sopaipillas. It's like getting woken up by a buttercup. Or a marigold. Or a chuparosa. Something lovely and wild that grows in the desert.

She summons us downstairs to do all the things responsible kids are supposed to do . . . little things like brush our teeth, take a shower, comb our hair, get dressed, and come down for breakfast. Today she is making chilaquiles, which means there is a rush to get to the table before Henry. Trust me. They're addictive. He has no guilt about polishing them off before I even get there.

But before we get down the attic stairs, Henry gives me a nudge.

"Eva, psst," he whispers. "I found something."

"What?"

He smiles, giddy. "That's for me to know and you to find out."

"Oh, c'mon. You're just saying that to stall me so that you get all the chilaquiles."

"Not this time." He winks. "After breakfast. You'll see."

"Fine."

Henry has a little zing in his shoe-step, just a little bounce to him he didn't have yesterday. Even if all of this turns out to be nonsense and he and I are both carted away to the funny farm babbling about ghosts, waterspouts, and gold miners, I find myself thinking that this little pep in my kid brother's previously heavy-with-the-weight-of-the-world step might be worth it.

3

BREAKFAST THIS MORNING mostly consists of Claude reading the real estate section of the *Los Angeles Times*, grumbling
to himself and then picking up the *Monterey Herald*. I think he
must be the only person left on earth who still reads an actual,
physical newspaper. Also, I think he must be the only person
left on earth who does not like chilaquiles.

Terri is looking intently at her phone the entire time. She
says it's super-duper important but I'm pretty sure she's playing
Candy Crush. Marisol is once again hiding in the other room,
this time glued to *Cosmos*. The new version, starring the guy
who wears the cool vests.

Henry is gloating into his chilaquiles, happy in the knowl-
edge he knows something I don't. He is, in fact, beaming for

the first time in a very long time.

This silent and excruciating breakfast seems to last forty years and then another forty years as Henry pours himself an uncharacteristic and unnecessary bowl of granola cereal.

"You already ate!" I whisper. "And you don't even like cereal!"

He smiles, whistling to himself, nonchalant.

"May we be excused, please?" I ask.

Terri doesn't look up. Claude glances up from a full-page ad on a Palm Springs golf property.

"Huh? Oh. Of course, kids. Have a . . . nice day." He sits there for a second, trying to think of something more original to say, then gives up, and goes back to his full-page ad.

Henry and I look at each other, then simultaneously bound up the stairs. It's three stories up to the attic and we are racing each other the whole way, at each turn trying to sneak our way in front of the other one.

He beats me on the stairs up to the attic by cutting me off on the landing.

"So annoying."

"Don't you mean 'such a mastermind'?" He mocks a diabolical gesture, throwing his head back in maniacal laughter. We're both giggling when we hear a click on the other side of the room and the sound of the audio, digitized, coming out over the computer, through all the speakers. The ghost in the machine.

It's the wailing sound we heard before, but without all the

crashing waves, sound of the surf, seagulls, and clicks from Henry's electromagnet-o-meter. We tiptoe inside, leaning in as the sound plays out the myriad speakers, wafting over the room like a mist, plaintive.

"Viiiiiiine. Theeeeeeeebooooooo!"

Henry and I look at each other.

"Viiiiiiiiiiiiiiine. Theeeeeeeeeeeeebooooooooooo!"

"What is it saying?" I whisper.

Henry looks at me, as quizzical as I am.

"I think it's saying . . . 'Vine Thebo'?"

"Well, what the heck is that supposed to mean?"

"Vine Thebo?!" Henry and I turn to see Plum plopped down below the marble run in all her spectral glory. Her feather fan flap-flaps away the dust.

"Sound like the name of some kind of hooch!" We spin around. This time it's Beaumont, the gold miner ghost, perched up next to the ladybug chalet, squinting in at the ladybugs.

August and Sturdevant blink into view close behind. "Obviously, it's some kind of fine wine. Perhaps from Château Pichon Longueville Baron in Bordeaux."

Each nods in agreement. "Quite, quite." They clink martini glasses.

"What does it matter what it means? The universe is a foul and unforgiving place, frequented by a series of meaningless, insignificant, desperate gestures on the inevitable, inescapable road to unending doom." That little piece of sunshine was brought to us by Maxine, draped over the window bench.

"Don't listen to Grumpy Gussy over here," Plum huffs. "I know exactly what it is! It's a clue!"

We all stare at each other.

"Your folks were trying to tell you something! It must have to do with the reason they"—she stops short, not wanting to be indelicate—"passed."

"But even then, what is it?" I ask. "What does it have to do with *how* they . . . passed?"

Plum snaps her incorporeal fingers. "I've got it! It's the name of a town. A town up the coast!" She stands up. "Let's all go."

"Nonsense, woman! I'm telling ya, it's moonshine, plain and simple!" Beaumont slaps his dungarees and dust flies everywhere, sending the entire room into coughing and sneezing spasms, including me and Henry.

"How about that?" Henry muses. "I'm even allergic to ghost dust."

"Um, excuse me, not to be rude, or even to seem ungrateful, but what, exactly, are you all doing back here?" I ask. "You told us what you needed to, so shouldn't you be off enjoying your own personal Ever Afters or what have you?"

"We could, but we're sticking around," Plum tells us.

Henry blinks. "But . . . why?"

"Why? We're helping you kids, of course! Just like we said." Plum smiles.

"Perhaps they don't want our help," August laments wistfully.

"Perhaps they don't need our help, old chum," echoes

Sturdevant, patting sad-faced August on the back.

"Perhaps life can be measured out in teacups and coffee spoons and the insipid minor existence of the masses who come and go like waves on a beach, each one insisting on its own importance. Know me. Acknowledge me. See me. But, alas, no one is to be seen," Maxine drones.

The entire room stares at her.

She looks up. "What? It's how I feel."

Henry shares a look with me, leans in.

"Eva, please pinch me. I need to renew my belief that this is actually happening, through scientific evidence."

I pinch him.

"Ow!! Thank you."

I roll my eyes.

"Kids! There's no time for your chicanery, skulduggery, and shenanigans! We must find a bottle of Vine Thebo! It must hold the key to the mystery!" Beaumont seems extremely excited about this heretofore unthought-of stash of liquor.

"Sounds enticing," August quips, nose in the air.

"Indeed." Sturdevant nods.

"We got a date with a bathtub of hooch hidden somewhere on this here property! The dearly departed of these here young-uns want us to find it!" Beaumont cheers.

"Now, now," Plum says, "I still think we should check a map. It might be a town up north, on the Oregon coast. Maybe past Eugene."

"'The undiscovered country from whose bourn no traveler returns, puzzles the will and makes us rather bear those ills we have than fly to others we know not of? Thus conscience doth make cowards of us all.'"

Again, the entire room falls silent.

"It's Shakespeare," Maxine says. "*Hamlet*, to be precise."

"Ah, the Bard." August and Sturdevant clink glasses respectfully.

"Dagnabbit. I can't take all this lily-livered lollygagging! We've got a Vine Thebo to open!"

But just as he's about to start a deluge of swearing and huffing and puffing over a probably nonexistent bottle of ancient whiskey, the attic trapdoor creaks and there is Marisol once again.

"The *Cosmos* has ended. Who are you two talking to up here in this spider place?"

Henry and I share a look, caught, and then look around us.

Crickets.

No one.

Not a single ghost.

Just the two of us in Henry's mad scientist laboratory.

And Marisol, who is looking at us like we are bonkers.

"Oh, we were just—"

"—practicing a play," I jump in.

"Yes, rehearsing. We were rehearsing a work of theater."

"Aha? And what is this play? This *obra de teatro*?"

"*The Sound of Music!*"

"*Sesame Street on Ice!*"

We blurt these out simultaneously.

"It's actually a version of *The Sound of Music on Ice*," I cover.

"I play the ice-skating, um, Nazi?" Henry offers. Then cringes.

I look at him.

He shrugs.

Marisol gives us the international look for "I don't believe you."

"Welp, this has all been great, Marisol, but I have to get back to memorizing my lines. Don't you? Henry? Don't you have to get ready to memorize your lines for *The Sound of Music* that we are rehearsing right now like we just said?"

"Yes, yes. Most certainly." Henry nods.

"*Doe, a deer, a female deer. Ray, a drop of golden sun . . .*" I'm singing now.

"*. . . Me, a name I call myself. Far, a long, long way to run . . .*" He joins in, a little flat, to be honest.

"*Sew! A needle pulling thread!*" I'm now doing a little impromptu dance number. Involving my arms in a kind of arch of a forward motion.

"*La! A note to follow sew!*" Henry is getting into it, following with his own hot moves.

Marisol just rolls her eyes and shuts the trapdoor.

SLAM!

"Well, that was a bit rude." Henry looks disappointed.

"I know. She could have at least waited until the end," I add.

Henry, dejected, laments, "People just don't appreciate theater like they used to."

THE ENDLESS NAUTICAL obsession of my dad on full display here, within the four walls of his office, might as well be the hull of a ship. On every centimeter of the wall behind his desk are nautical paintings of ships in every kind of weather. A ship at dawn. A ship in a storm. A ship carved out of a wooden board. And then there are the whale teeth, etched in scrimshaw. And the glass display of a variety of sailor knots. And the steering wheel, from a boat sunk off the coast of Maine in 1743. On the top of his desk, a ship in a bottle, its three sails raised high and the string rigging intricate, each line perfectly placed.

There is mahogany paneling up to the navy-blue-painted walls, covered in high-seas art. And even two gray stools, washed up from the beach. They look like the spine of some long-forgotten whale.

Right now we are trying to break into my dad's desk. Mission: uncover anything relating to "Vine Thebo."

Plum's excused herself for the moment (some sort of ghostly duties to attend to?) and although I appreciate her enthusiasm, the experience of spending time with ghosts, even friendly ones, is . . . unsettling.

The ghosts were certainly giving it their all, but I'm not sure they were, exactly, helpful.

"Vine Thebo" could be anything. Maybe a lake, or a map, or a map of a lake. You get the idea.

There is a little key to the cherrywood monolith that is our dad's desk. It's somewhere, but no one knows where it is. This is where Henry's uncanny mechanical skills come in handy. I'm pretty sure if he thinks long enough about it, he can break into anything.

"Do you think we'll get in trouble for this?" I ask.

"With who. Terri the Terrible? I don't think she even knows what a study is, let alone that there's one in this house."

"True." I think about it. "But maybe Claude does."

CLUNK. The desk lock opens.

"Wait? How did you do that?"

He holds up a bobby pin, proud. "The magic of friction."

The drawer slides out and inside there are papers stacked on papers stacked on files stacked on receipts stacked on maps stacked on photographs. Same for the side drawers. Same for the bottom drawers. Same for the top drawers.

"So, organization was not our dad's strong suit."

"Wow. Okay. This is going to take forever."

Somehow seeing all the detritus from his desk deflates me. What is left? What is left when you go? This? A drawer full of papers? A few receipts? A host of old, possibly unpaid bills? A parking ticket? What does it all mean? All these numbers on papers and wanting for things? All this red tape and correspondence and paperwork? What is all this trying even for?

Oh no, I sound like Maxine.

"All right. Let's just concentrate on finding the words 'Vine' or 'Thebo' or both in any of these papers. I'll take this side. I think it's only fair you take that side."

Henry is not allowing himself this moment of existential doubt. He is on a mission. It's true, he's always been very goal-oriented. A vector. Henry needs a vector. Not waddling around. Not chitchat. A quest. A goal. There always has to be forward motion.

The problem is that nearly six hours later, this mission is not complete. Nothing is accomplished.

What we have is an epic fail.

Henry and I sit here, on the ground, engulfed in papers. We have found not one single reference, not one tiny, itty-bitty scrap of paper with the words "Vine" or "Thebo" on it. Our eyes are bloodshot from the strain and by now the sun is dipping down, making squares through the dormers. Little pieces of light, catching the dust motes in the room, which seem to be increasing every minute.

Henry sneezes.

"Okay, I think we may have to consider looking somewhere else. Henry?"

He exhales, sitting back into a pile of papers as tall as a sofa.

"I mean, do you really think we're going to find it here? We've been searching since ten in the morning. It's four o'clock. See?"

I point to the clock on Dad's desk. A clock shaped like a ship's wheel, carved in maple.

Henry looks up at the clock. Then, next to it, the miniature SS *Constellation* in a bottle. His face is turned down and the failure of this quest is starting to weigh on his shoulders. Down down down he slumps into the netherworld of paperwork beneath.

We both sit silent for a moment, the only sound the call of a California towhee somewhere outside in the trees. *Chirp . . . chirp . . . chirp . . . chirp chirp chirpchirp.* Then a stop. *Chirp . . . chirp . . . chirp . . . chirp chirp chirpchirp.* It's a funny little call, accelerating and then abruptly stopping. As if it forgot what it was so angry about in the first place.

And we are stopped, too. Sitting here in this amber-sunlit room. Stopped abruptly but not forgetting. Never forgetting.

Suddenly Henry's face is lit up from inside and he stands up. Looking at the tiny SS *Constellation* trapped in the yellowing glass bottle.

He stands there, wheels turning in his head, the way they've always whirled with him.

"Eva. We're idiots."

"Well, I wouldn't call us *idiots*. I'd just say we're at the beginning of a process, and life, as a process full of moments, is what lends wisdom to—"

"No, *we're idiots*."

"Jeez. Honestly, are you trying to hurt my feelings—"

"There's no person named Vine Thebo."

"Wait. What?"

"There is no place named Vine Thebo, either."

"There isn't?"

"That's not what it was on the audio. It just sounded like that, with all the wind and the waves crashing against the rocks taken out. It just sounded like that with no accounting for the echo or the reverberation against the rocks and the ocean tide."

"Well . . . um . . . I'm not confused at all. Also, what?"

"It just *sounded* like 'Vine Thebo,' but I believe the words really were . . ."

"Um, I'm waiting . . ."

"Find. The. Boat."

My mouth drops open.

Now *that*, dear readers, sounds like a clue!

5

SO, TO MAKE sure you've got this all firmly in your head:

Two months ago, my parents died.

Since then my father's brother and his terrible girlfriend moved into our house.

As of this week, we have learned not only that ghosts are real but that my long-lost family members have risen from their eternal slumber to deliver a message to us that our dead parents couldn't. A message that *could* lead to evidence that my parents were not the victims of a tragic accident but *foul play*.

That message was "FIND THE BOAT." The boat that they sank in, which was never recovered.

You good? All caught up? Okay.

So, the next morning, in our room, we decide to come up

with a plan to, you guessed it, find the boat.

"Oh my God. We are so stupid. Vine Thebo. I feel so dumb."

"You are not alone," Henry reassures me.

The weight of this new discovery is still hitting us when the sound of footsteps comes toward us, creaking the floorboards down the hall.

KNOCK KNOCK KNOCK

Henry and I look at each other.

"Morning, you two!"

It's Claude. Not another ghost invasion. Somehow this is a relief.

"I thought we could take the day and you guys could see what I do to pay the bills. You know, come along with your old uncle. *Take your kids to work day.*"

Henry and I share a moment of disbelief.

He opens his mouth but I stop him. I know what he's going to say. Henry wants to say, "We're not your kids." But that doesn't seem helpful.

"Um . . . what?" That's me.

Living with Claude has been kind of like living with a rump roast. He's just . . . there. So why the sudden . . . engagement?

"I thought it'd be fun! You know, see the office. You'll love it. It's all glass! Designed by Renzo Piano. They even put it in *Sunset* magazine!"

I look at Henry, who is shaking his head.

"Uuuuummmm . . ."

Henry leans in, whispers, "Negative. We cannot be tied up.

We have to *find the boat*."

"Look, I think it will be exciting! I'll even buy you an ice cream. Or a frozen yogurt. Or whatever weird almond-soy-cruelty-free thing the kids are eating these days."

Henry has two eyes that are normally eye-size but at this moment are as big as geodes.

He's trying to beam the word "NO" into my skull and out of my mouth.

But I am curious.

"Okay, yeah, sure, whatever, Uncle Claude."

"You realize that's not a sentence, don't you?" Henry responds, dire.

"Great, kids! I'll just go get some piping hot, and wheels up in half an hour! How's that sound?"

"Uh, sure, yeah. Wheels up in thirty minutes!"

"Piping hot?" Henry squints at me.

"I think he means coffee," I whisper back.

"Should I invite Terri?"

"NO!" We say this simultaneously.

Claude chuckles. "Well, all right then. Just us."

"Poke, you owe me a Coke," I whisper, poking Henry, who rolls his eyes.

"Do you know that you are, like, a professional eye-roller?" I ask.

Now the footsteps disappear down the hall. They're not really footsteps as much as whole-house-shaking steps. Claude is a big man. And he carries himself like a big man. He definitely needs to work on his core. It's stomp city over here.

"Do you think he picked up on our Terri-dislike?"

Henry thinks.

"It's hard to say. On the one hand, he seems completely oblivious. On the other hand, it would require a certain amount of sensitivity, which Uncle Claude seems to lack."

"Do you think *he* likes Terri?"

"On a scale of one to ten . . . one being apathy and ten being obsession . . . I would say he's about a . . . six."

"I was gonna say six!" Somehow this makes me proud. "In any case, if memory serves, I believe there's a little item of interest to our mutual cause nearly adjacent to the office tower of a certain Uncle Claude 'the Clod' Billings."

"Okay, what is it?"

"Gee, maybe I'll make you wait to find out. You love a riddle. And right now, I need to get dressed. And take a shower. And possibly wash my hair."

"You never wash your hair."

"What? Why would you say that?"

"You just never do. Unless it's an emergency."

"Well, my arms get tired. But that's not the point. This time *I* get to gloat. Unless you guess."

"What? No."

"Guess."

"No."

"Guess!"

"No!"

"Okay, fine."

"What is it?!"

"*It*, my dear brother, is a marina. A marina named Breakwater Cove. The selfsame marina where Mom and Dad kept . . ."

We say the last part together.

". . . the boat."

6

UNCLE CLAUDE'S PLACE is head-to-toe glass. It's everywhere. I mean, you practically expect the floors to be glass, too. There is even an atrium in the middle of all four stories, with a giant eucalyptus tree growing out of it, creating the feeling of being in a forest and, also, the smell of being in the bathtub.

There's no other way to say it. It's beautiful. And modern. And open. And airy. Renzo Piano, the architect, was not phoning it in. I find myself shocked, nay, bewildered, that this place could have been built under the watchful eye of its CEO, Claude Shaw Billings, aka our uncle, aka someone who wears sports jerseys.

"See, kids, over there, you can see all the way out on the ocean. Here, I have some binoculars up here in my office.

Sometimes you can even see the whales out there. I'm not sure what kind of whales—"

"Humpback whales. Or possibly the California gray whale. Between November and April. In their annual migration to Mexico."

These words are coming out of Henry's mouth but his mind is elsewhere, looking at each nook, bolt, beam of this sparkling glass office building, to analyze exactly how it's constructed.

"How is this retrofitted?" It's a question to Claude, whose answer is a blank stare.

"There's ice cream in the kitchen, kids!" This is, also, an appropriate answer.

I was expecting the kitchen to be tucked away in a little corner with someone's frozen Smart Choice Sweet & Sour Teriyaki Chicken hidden away with a proprietary note on it. (Why was I expecting this? The magic of film! Whenever you see an office in a film it always looks like a total depression zone. Papers everywhere. Files. Charcoal-colored cubicles with the odd family picture clipped somewhere. Someone's name always tacked to the fridge food.)

But this is not that kind of office.

Even the kitchen is a consciously lit affair with a juice bar, vegan tacos, and sushi.

Sushi! With a man behind a counter *fashioning* said sushi.

I'm not kidding, I think that he is now rolling an actual sushi burrito. Yes. It exists. A sushi burrito. Greatest thing to sweep the coast since the Korean taco. Don't be jealous.

The seating area is playful, with slumping, comfortable sofas and chairs everywhere, little semicircles, ready for invigorating conversations between people who have not yet arrived. Constructive lunch talk! Inspired juice bar musing! Sushi burrito brainstorming!

"How awkward is the conversation, generally, between the people who work here?"

Henry's question may seem tangential but it's essentially because he's picturing himself in this environment and ascertaining whether he would like it.

"What? Oh, um. It's . . . nice, I guess." Claude has clearly never thought of this before.

Henry contemplates for a second. "I guess if you're the CEO it doesn't matter because people have to like you. So it would be difficult to analyze without a control in the experiment. Like a fake boss. Or a CEO masquerading in some sort of disguise—"

I elbow Henry. Claude just pretends not to hear.

"Uncle Claude, what Henry is saying is that it's a beautiful space."

"What? No, that's not what I was—"

Again, I elbow him, accompanied by *a look*.

It's not Henry's fault, you know. He just has a slightly different way of thinking and, therefore, communicating. And no edit button.

"Well, that's nice, kids. And up here is . . . my office!"

He pauses, in order to let us take in the magic.

No need for snark here. This is just straight-up amazing with views 360 degrees around, including oceans and cliffs and, possibly, humpback whales in the distance. They might as well be swimming in a circle and singing.

"See, it's the whole floor!" Claude boasts. "That way I can run laps if I don't have time to go to the gym." He winks.

Henry is in the corner now, looking up at the crossbeams.

"Ah, I see! It's a facade retrofit."

This revelation seems to temporarily elate Henry, before he begins looking at the crossbeams in the ceiling and then continuing the mumbled conversation he's been having with himself and the ten different engineers in his head.

Claude just looks at me.

"He's very curious," I assure him.

There are a lot of questions I have for Claude right now. Questions like . . . Why are you being so nice to us? What are we doing here? Who *are* you and what have you done with our actual uncle? But Claude doesn't seem to be the kind of guy who actually responds to or acknowledges the human reality on the ground, so . . . I stick to small talk.

"So, um, how long did it take to build this?"

"Oh, heck, I think it's been about . . . five years now, maybe six. Time flies so fast I just never know these days!"

A voice comes over the intercom. "Mr. Billings, I have Redwood Global Capital on the line."

"Oh, jeez! Can you kids give me a sec—"

Before he finishes his sentence, he's out of the room.

And before I begin my next sentence, Henry starts his.

"Look. Look down there. Do you see it?"

He points to a room, made of glass, the next floor down.

"I can't really tell what you're pointing at."

"That . . . that diorama."

I squint, looking around. Everything just seems like a mass of industriousness, movement, and glass.

"Here, I'll show you."

Henry goes flying down the see-through staircase, down the see-through hallway, and into a see-through room, which, although it is totally transparent, somehow seems like a secret.

"There."

There, indeed. There, over on the other side of the room, is a diorama of a behemoth white condo complex, perched ominously over the sea, set high up on a cliff.

"Wait a minute. Are you kidding me right now?" I say, taking it in.

"I'm afraid the joke is on us."

We both stare down at the enormous, high ivory towers, dwarfing everything around them. Could it really be that Uncle Claude is planning on building this monstrosity on the side of a cliff, overlooking the ocean? And, more important, could it really be that he's planning on building this monstrosity on the side of *our* cliff? Because this . . . this sure looks like our cliff. The one where our house sits. You know, the one that's been in the family since 1850?

Why would he do that? Would he do that? *Who would do that?*

As if on cue, Claude pops his head in.

"Hey, you crazy kids, what are you up to in—"

But he is stopped when he sees the diorama. Actually, he is stopped seeing Henry's sunken face looking at the diorama.

"Uhh . . . isn't she a beaut?" he says, nodding to the miniature white condo towers. "They say it's gonna fetch a pretty penny. I mean, once it's built, of course."

"Uncle Claude, where, exactly, is this going . . . ?" I can't help myself.

"Where? Well, it's going . . . um, it's going . . . down the coast somewhere. El Cajon."

"El Cajon is in a valley surrounded by mountains," Henry corrects him.

Leave it to Henry to know everything about every inland community in the state of California.

"Right! But this is *West* El Cajon . . . which is, I guess, well, in fact . . . San Diego."

"West El Cajon?"

"Yes, West El Cajon."

Henry and I share a look of disbelief.

"Why? Where did you think it was going?" Claude asks, still smiling.

Henry shakes his head at me. He wants me to drop it.

"Nowhere! It's just, um, we were curious. That's all." I smile.

"Huh. Okay, kids, we should probably get going, so—"

"Oh, I forgot! We have a summer camp science class! In marine biology!" Henry blurts out. "We signed up for it last

April. It was pretty expensive. So . . . do you think you can just drop us off at the marina?"

"The marina?"

"Yes, Breakwater Cove, sir. We have a marine mammal class. It's part of this whole summer camp fun thing they do," he adds.

"Well, I don't remember anybody mentioning anything about—" Claude seems befuddled.

"Oh, it's just some dumb thing we signed up for, like, a year ago. No biggie. It's just a one-day camp. Like a workshop. We'll be home by dinner even. We could bring home dinner, if you want! There's a great fish place right there . . ." I continue the charade.

"Neptune's Net. It's named after the god of the sea. The Roman god, of course. The Greek god is Poseidon, obviously." Henry can't help himself.

"Right. Well, I'll have my assistant, Moira, drop you off then. I have a few more phone calls . . ." Claude steps out of the room.

"Great!" I say with unnatural enthusiasm.

And this would all work perfectly well and fine and peachy except, halfway to Moira's vehicle, Claude comes running out of the glass building, huffing and puffing as if this may be the first time he's run in ten years, and announces, "Wait! Did you say you were going to Breakwater Cove?"

"Um . . . yes." Henry and I both look at each other.

"Well, I really don't think that's a good idea for you to go alone. It's . . . not safe."

"We won't be alone, it's, like, a day camp."

Claude peers at us . . . This is a look I remember coming from my mother.

"So, you're telling me you kids are randomly taking an ocean class where you have to just show up at a dock by yourselves and nobody told me about it?"

"Kind of." It's all I can muster. "We just didn't really think you'd care that much."

Henry is looking at an ant trail in the parking lot, trying to figure out where it starts. There are a lot of ants involved. A row stretching out over the curb and into the grass.

"Sorry, kids. But something seems fishy here."

"Literally." Henry can't help himself.

"Look, I don't know what you kids have planned, but I didn't just fall off the cabbage truck," Claude asserts.

"Look, Uncle Claude. We just forgot to tell you. It's a day camp. Involving sea creatures. It's no big deal! And we really have been looking forward to it . . ." I give him my world-patented puppy eyes. "Mom signed us up for it before . . . well, you know."

Uncle Claude stands there, contemplating. "Well, okay. I guess I'll go get my keys. But *I'm* the one dropping you off. Just to be sure. You are my responsibility, you know." He marches back toward the glass-diamond building. When he's inside, Henry turns to me—

"Cabbage truck?"

"I think it means we're not fooling him."

"So, there was a time when people were riding around on cabbage trucks and, apparently, the ones who fell off weren't that intelligent."

"I guess." I shrug.

"Why cabbage?"

"Maybe it just didn't sound as good to say 'fell off the cucumber truck.'"

"Do you think there was such a thing as a cucumber truck?"

"Why not?"

"It doesn't make sense to just have one vegetable per truck. They should diversify," Henry points out.

Sure, they should.

And *we* should be hot on the heels of some answers. As soon as Claude returns with the keys to his Lexus.

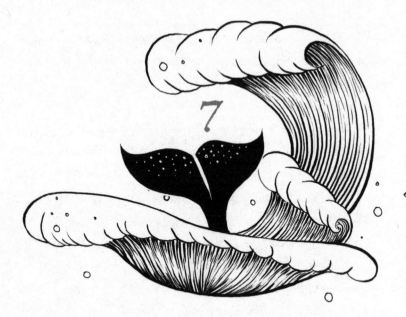

IT'S STILL EARLY afternoon by the time we make it to Break-water Cove. Claude seems to be obsessed with the idea that if we don't see our completely imaginary marine mammal instructor, he's just not dropping us off. I have no idea where this newfound paternal instinct comes from. Maybe old Clod has a heart after all . . . just a quiet one that likes to warble on about real estate and not draw attention to itself.

"There!" Henry points to a squat woman in a straw sun hat. "There she is! That's our marine biology instructor! Her name is . . . Ruth."

Claude sizes her up from a distance. "Ruth, huh?"

She definitely looks straight out of central casting for marine mammal science instructor. Sturdy clogs, batik ankle-length skirt in a tie-dyed wave pattern, black T-shirt, wiry gray hair. Nice one, Henry.

Claude sizes her up. "Where are the rest of the kids?"

I clear my throat. "Well, I'm pretty sure it's a small class. And we're early, so . . ."

I know. I am *so* fast on my feet.

"Well, okay. Fine. But be back before sunset, kids. I mean it"—he nods, keeping the noble-dad act going—"or *Ruth* and I are going to have words."

As we hop out, Henry runs over to the pretend science teacher. I really have to wonder what he is planning on saying to her, considering the situation.

Claude stays, idling the car—waiting to see us make contact, making sure we're not up to something. But what could *he* possibly think we're up to?

By the time I catch up, Henry and the woman are having an honest-to-goodness conversation about shellfish.

"That's interesting, son. I never knew that oysters change their gender at least once in their lifetime!" She looks down on Henry sweetly.

"That's not all, ma'am. They have astounding nutritional value, including vitamins C, D, B1, B2, and B3. If you were to eat four oysters a day you would get the recommended daily value for calcium, copper, iodine, iron, magnesium, manganese, phosphorus, and zinc!"

I look back to Claude idling in the car and give him a thumbs-up. He squints, still dubious, then reverses the car and drives off.

Wow. I guess we fooled him.

I have to give it to Henry, he really knows how to pick imaginary sea instructors.

"Well, thank you for your time, ma'am. I enjoyed sharing the magic of the seven seas with you." Henry bows and walks off briskly, leaving the woman looking a bit befuddled. I guess she thought he was going to stick around spouting facts all day.

By the time I catch up with Henry, he's already at the end of the dock, speaking with a middle-aged man with reddish-blond hair, wearing a beige polo.

"Sir, is this your boat?" Henry asks. "I see it has sonar equipment."

And, indeed, behind the man, on the hull of the medium-size motorboat, is an array of gunmetal-gray boxes, filled with screens, knobs, and switches.

"Sure is, kid. It's not much, but I like to pride myself on it. Took a while to put together the system. I did it myself, you know." There's a kind of affable quality about this ginger-haired captain.

"Do you ever rent it out, sir?"

The man's demeanor changes. He's a nice man, the kind you'd find trustworthy. His accent sounds almost Australian but not quite.

"I do, as a matter of fact. But it's quite expensive. Too

expensive for you kids, I'm afraid," he laments.

"Well, how much is it?" I ask.

"Depends. On the kind of folks making the offer, mostly."
Then he whispers, "If they're from San Francisco, I double the
price."

Henry and I nod, in cahoots.

"What are you kids looking for, eh? A little whale watching?
Maybe a dolphin? Some seals, perchance?"

Henry looks up at him, pauses. "Actually, we're looking for
our parents' boat. It fell to the bottom of the ocean."

Of course, this stops the light little conversation in its tracks.
The man's face drops and he looks at the two of us like we are
the last feral dogs left at the pound.

"They died. Our parents. At sea. Sorry to bother you," I
mutter.

Henry and I turn to walk away, both of us slumped forward,
not wanting to be looked at in that way. Like things to be pitied.

We're halfway down the dock when we hear his voice calling behind us.

"Hey! Hey! I know you. Your parents . . . they were the
Billingses, yeah?"

We nod.

"They were on this pier. Good people." He rubs the stubble
on his chin. "Well, I'm sure a little afternoon outing wouldn't
hurt anyone, eh? Climb aboard. We'll see what we can see."

8

THE BOAT IS slicing through the whitecaps at fantastic speed. The wind whips my hair back from my shoulders, and the salt air makes the skin on my face feel washed clean.

"Like it?" our captain asks. "I named her the *Esmerelda Jane*! After my ex-girlfriend who I broke up with. Well, actually, she broke up with me."

We're racing along the Pacific coast, due southwest, and the rusty-haired captain in the beige polo has been talking essentially the entire time.

His name is Wayne. He's from New Zealand.

"Mostly, I just came to the States on a lark, really! Just wanted to see the world, find my way, eh!"

Henry and I are standing next to him, holding tight to the

rails, the wind whipping our faces and the boat bucking up and down through the waves.

"If you start to feel a bit nauseous I've got some wristbands for that, then! Pressure points! Get you tip-top in no time!"

There's no question there's something engaging about this slightly goofy yet extremely friendly captain we find ourselves crashing through the ocean waves with.

"Here. Latitude: North 36° 15'51.1445 Longitude: West 121° 51'59.5129. This was the last transmission."

Fun fact: I don't want to think about that. Those words. *Last transmission.*

Wayne looks back at Henry. "Let's slow down then, eh?"

The motor putters down and the endless bouncing calms down to more of a bobble. Wayne turns on the sonar equipment and now there's a ping. *Ping.* Pause. *Ping.* Pause. As the sonar tries to detect what's underneath, drawing a picture from the seafloor, the three of us strain to decipher the blips and beeps.

"So, they lost the boat, then? The Coast Guard?" Wayne asks over the breeze off the bow.

"Yeah. They said they couldn't find anything," I answer.

"I don't see how that is." He frowns. "Accident at sea— there'd still be something. There are *pirate wrecks* down in Davy Jones's locker, for Pete's sake. And those vessels're made of wood! Your parents' boat—fiberglass. It seems to me they should have looked a bit harder."

Henry nods. "That's why we're here."

Our captain sets his lips in a grim line. He seems determined to help. Or he may be certain that if the Coast Guard didn't find anything, we sure as heck won't. Hard to tell.

He mans his gunmetal-gray boxes, turning this knob, flicking that switch.

It's about one and a half hours later when we hear it. *PING.* Somewhere below, the sonar equipment is detecting something on the oceanbed.

Henry and Wayne rush to the equipment to begin to suss it out.

"Oh, looky, there," Wayne says, interpreting the readouts. "That's about three foot by two foot."

Henry nods. "How deep?"

"We're not in the canyon. Not here. Probably only about fifty feet."

I shudder. *Only* fifty feet? Fifty feet of water above one's head sounds frightening. It sounds heavy. It sounds impossible.

The two of them stand there, making it out, imagining the exact shape and dimensions.

"You said it's about three by two feet, yes?" Henry asks.

"Yeah, that's right, I suppose," Wayne replies. "But you know, there's really only one sure way to find out."

"How?" I ask.

Wayne reaches into a storage bin on the boat's deck and pulls out a wet suit. He winks. "We go and get it."

Thankfully, by "we," Wayne means "he." Henry and I are watching from the relative safety of the boat as he floats in the water, adjusting his mask and his regulator, which is attached to the giant tank of oxygen on his back. "Now don't you worry," he calls up to us. "I'm an expert diver. Dove the Great Barrier Reef more times than I can count. This is nothing but a nice little swim. Be back in a jif!"

Henry waves, and Wayne slips below the surface.

A few bubbles fizz in Wayne's wake—and then silence.

Henry and I stare at the spot in the water, waiting.

The lines clank against the metal mast.

A gull cries in the distance.

"He's not coming back, is he?" I ask.

"Of course he's coming back," Henry answers crabbily.

A wave slaps against the ship's aft deck. We rock ever so gently.

"But hypothetically if he doesn't return then we—"

"Eva!"

I don't understand why Henry won't consider the possibility and help me come up with a plan. I mean, considering the reason why we're here, it seems like the responsible thing to do.

Instead, he's just fixed on that spot in the sea, willing Captain Wayne to the surface by the force of his gaze.

My stomach growls. Would we starve out here? Henry is inventive. He'd find a way to catch and cook something. I consider all the variety of food swimming just below our hull. I wonder if Henry would be able to coax a Dungeness crab aboard. We could make him our pet. Name him Pinchy . . .

I let out a yawn. Perhaps I should lie down. I wonder if it's possible to lounge anywhere on this ship while I—

SPLASH!

"Ahoy!" a voice yells. Captain Wayne has returned. And he's holding something that looks like a medium-size black bag over his head. Now he takes something out, hands it to me.

I gaze down at the hunk of metal in my hands. "What is it?" I ask.

"Eva, don't you see?" Henry asks.

I turn it over, and then I know.

"Mom kept forgetting where she docked the boat. And Dad kept teasing her about getting mixed up and walking around and around the piers forever like a crazy person," Henry says, spelling it out for me.

This is true. Our mother was a space cadet. She had an extremely difficult time remembering where she put things. Anything. Keys, glasses, remotes, phones, cars, boats, herself. I must have spent at least an entire month of my life, altogether, searching around for her car in various parking structures. She became so frustrated she actually had a mini Poseidon sculpture specially made and welded to the boat. That was her genius and slightly offbeat solution. Which was remarkably successful, by the way.

"It's him," I say. Mini Poseidon now sits in my hands, as if just emerging from the sea, trident in hand, covered in intricate sculptured seaweed. None of us liked the sculpture, quite honestly. Dad said it was pretentious. Henry said it was creepy. I just thought it looked kind of hideous, like a wrongly placed hood ornament. But Mom would always defend it.

Except now . . . the trident he is holding is somehow bent backward. As if Zeus himself blew a godlike wind, bending the tines of the trident like a wax fork.

"That trident took a bit of a beating, yeah?" Wayne asks.

I nod to Wayne. "Yes. It's bent. But how would that even . . ."

Henry stays looking at the bent cast trident, analyzing.

"The statue is made entirely of metal. Nothing could do that. Except . . ." Henry stops, breathing in.

Suddenly everything is quiet. Even the sea shushes its waves.

Wayne and Henry share a look.

"And if this is here," I ask, "where is the rest of the boat?"

Wayne goes silent.

Henry turns to me. "Eva, I think you should sit down."

Wayne pretends to be nonchalant, engaged in something having to do with returning his dive equipment to its proper place.

"Why should I sit down? Henry? What is it? Just say it."

"Just brace yourself, okay. You are not going to like what I'm about to say." This is a quiet kind of Henry. Flushed and brooding.

Now Wayne has completely disappeared to the aft side of the deck.

Henry exhales, puts his arms on my shoulders, and looks deep into my eyes.

"Eva, there's only one way the trident on that miniature Poseidon statue could be bent back like that while everything else, besides the metal sonar equipment, is completely missing from the ocean floor."

"What is that, Henry?" I'm bracing myself now, too.

He pauses for a second, taking in the azure chop of the waves.

"An explosion."

9

PRETTY MUCH THE entire way back to the marina there is utter silence. Even Wayne, the gregarious New Zealander, has decided there's really nothing to say. Nothing worth saying. I don't blame him. What would you say to two kids who just found out their parents were killed by an explosion?

And the questions, the myriad of questions. *Was it* an accident? If not, who would do this, and why? What possible kind of lost, ruthless soul would do something like this to a marine mammal rescuer and an environmental scientist? Not just a husband and wife but the parents of two children? The parents of . . . us.

I'll admit it. There was part of me, a little but not unsubstantial part, that was hoping all these ghost shenanigans and that

Vine Thebo hullabaloo would end up signifying nothing more than a pile of lima beans. It hadn't occurred to me that all of this might actually add up to something significant. Like a bomb.

Even though Henry isn't speaking I can hear the gears in his head grinding, backing up, starting again, twirling, whirring, humming. He's going through it, too. Every angle. Every question. Every outcome.

As we near the marina, a battalion of empty masts sticks up toward the heavens, hundreds of white toothpicks bobbing and swaying under the now-darkening sky.

"Henry, if we are so sure it was an explosion, should we call the police?"

Henry thinks. "Maybe we need more evidence. We don't know what actually happened. We have to assume the authorities will just think we are dumb kids, grasping at straws."

"But what if we—"

"Eva, I think we have to make it . . . credible. Oftentimes police can be persuaded by their own bias. And against kid investigators who are mourning their parents' passing? There is definitely a bias."

"Henry, this isn't *Law and Order*. It's Mom and Dad!"

"I know. But we just don't know enough yet. That's my instinct."

We lock eyes and I know he's right. The police would probably just shrug us off at this point. After all, this is Big Sur. Not Scotland Yard.

When we finally reach the dock, Wayne helps us out of the

boat with what appears to be extra tenderness. A tenderness I assume is reserved for orphans created by foul play.

"Now you kids take care of yourselves, you hear? Anything you need, just don't hesitate to call old Uncle Wayne here! Not that I'm your uncle. I don't know why I said that. Mostly I just meant a person who had a warm relationship to you in a way that wasn't your own parent or a complete stranger because that would be weird, wouldn't it?"

Despite everything, Henry and I can't help but smile at this affable SCUBA man, from the land Down Under where all those hobbits hail from.

"We will. We'll take care," Henry replies.

"And thank you," I add, nodding.

Looking back at him, there on the dock, I can't help but think there can be kindness in the world, a secret kindness like the current of a butterfly's wings, and if you blink you could miss it.

10

IT'S SUNSET BY the time we get home and that is why the person, sitting in the kitchen with his back to us, is nothing more than a black silhouette. There, standing in front of him, leaning on the counter, sizing him up, is Marisol. She is not impressed.

Whoever is there, he has long, medium-brown hair and a backpack, and definitely, most definitely, needs a shower.

Henry and I stand in the doorway looking at this mysterious figure in silhouette. I'm not sure if I can take any more ghosts today, so I am hoping this is an actual carbon-based life-form.

The heavy footsteps of Uncle Claude creak the floors upstairs as he comes down the endless hallway to the landing. Now it's his turn to see the mysterious silhouetted figure.

"Finn?!" Claude steps down from the landing. "What are *you* doing here?"

The silhouette turns, stands, and does a kind of mock bow back to Claude.

"That's me. In the flesh, maestro."

Henry and I stand still in the doorway, not knowing how to take this. Finn? As in our *uncle* Finn? Globe-trotting, world-saving, authentic-experience-having Uncle Finn?

Let's see. Straggly hair, Birkenstocks, weird toes, bad smells, happy faces, the vague smell of patchouli. I mean . . . maybe?

Straggly Hair sees us in the doorway.

"Hey, little dudes! Don't you remember me? Your uncle Finn? I sent you a postcard from Machu Picchu or was it Rajasthan or maybe it was Kathmandu. I mean, it's not like any of those places is exactly known for their mail delivery, although I'd put my money on Machu Picchu, if I were betting or something, but why would I be betting on that, that would be a strange thing to bet on. Like, who would bet on that? Only a psychopath!"

Henry, Claude, Marisol, and I stand flummoxed by this monologue.

Marisol rolls her eyes from beside the fridge.

"But, like, if I had known there was such a beautiful *mamacita chula* here, I would have visited, like, years ago," he says, winking at Marisol.

"Don't talk to me." Wow. Marisol is not having it.

She seems extremely suspicious, which is odd. She's usually

much warmer. Maybe Marisol is allergic to hippies.

Our long-lost uncle steps in close, earnest. "But honestly, kids. I came as soon as I got the news. Not the best signal where I was, actually. But I hopped immediately on a puddle jumper to Ulan, then to Seoul, then on an actual plane to Narita—that's Tokyo—up to SF, then hitched a ride down here with the dude sitting next to me on the plane. Interesting guy. Import-export business. Not bad for a suit. No offense, Claude."

Uncle Claude looks unamused.

I step in. "Uncle Finn! Of course! Nice to see you." This is all I can come up with. Pretty basic.

"You, too, you little scamp! You little guys are growing up so fast!"

Henry hides behind me, and I don't blame him. We haven't really interacted much with this particular uncle. He was always off somewhere in the jungles of Peru trying to find the Lost City of Zed or acclimating himself in a Nepalese base camp beneath Mount Everest with a Sherpa around, probably super annoyed with him. Quite frankly, my dad had pretty much given up on Uncle Finn ever coming back to the States. Sometimes he'd just say he ran off to join the circus. This would usually be followed by a barely perceptible eye roll.

Claude stands aloof, contemplating his little brother's presence with only a hint of politeness.

"Huh." He pauses. "It's great to see you, little brother. Here."

Uncle Claude gives scraggly Uncle Finn the most awkward hug the world has ever known. It looks like two elephant seals

trying to get their fins around each other. A lot of back patting/
stiff hand flapping.

"Right on, dude. Good to see you, too!" Uncle Finn holds
on a little too long. This must be how they hug in Kalamazoo.

"So how, um, have . . . you . . . been?" Claude ekes out.

"Look, man . . . like I said, I heard the news . . ." Uncle Finn
replies, shaking his head, turning to us with tenderness. "About
your dad. And your mom. I'm so sorry, man. I just . . . I just
wish I'd been here. Wish I'd come home sooner . . ."

And now he's crying.

Honestly, our prodigal Uncle Finn just broke down crying.
And not wistful tears that he's trying to hold in. No, no. Giant,
blubbering tears, spewing all over the place. And now he's col-
lapsing into Uncle Claude's uncomfortable arms.

"It's okay, buddy. Try to keep it together." Then Claude
whispers, "Hey, not in front of the kids, okay?"

Uncle Finn looks up, puzzled, then understands. Oh, yeah, a
normal adult does not completely break down in front of little
children. Right.

"Okay, okay. I got it. Sorry, kids. I'm just . . . emotional, I
guess. Tired from the journey."

"Where did you come from exactly?" Henry's natural state
is curiosity.

"Ulaanbaatar."

"Mongolia! Land of the Eternal Blue Sky! Two hundred and
fifty-seven cloudless days a year. Did you see the Gobi Desert?
What was it like? Were you able to distinguish between the

desert and the Gobi terrain or did it all look similar to you as a Westerner?"

Because Henry.

"Wow, little dude. Most kids your age couldn't pick Ulaanbaatar out on a map."

"Ridiculous! It's only the Mongol Empire, the largest contiguous land empire in world history," Henry informs me. I nod. Of course.

"Well, this has been great, kids," Uncle Claude interrupts. "But if you don't mind I'd like to have a moment in private with my kid brother, your uncle here. Marisol, do you mind taking the kids upstairs for a moment, please?"

Marisol obliges and the three of us march out of the room, turning the corner, stomping up the staircase, and then, immediately, tiptoeing back down the staircase to take our rightful place in eavesdropping position.

"You have no right being here," Claude whispers.

"Says you! *Vulture*," Finn snaps back.

"Dropout."

"Capitalist!"

"Failure." Claude lands that last one like a knockout.

Marisol, Henry, and I look at each other, wide-eyed. Our parents never spoke to anyone like this, least of all family.

"What's wrong, Finn? Got chased out of Helsinki? Bet on the wrong horse in Dubai? You make me sick. Stay away from these kids!" Claude barks.

"Ha!" Uncle Finn scoffs. "You're one to talk. I bet you've

been buttering them up good, huh?"

The three of us freeze in the stairwell.

Henry whispers what we're all thinking. "Buttering us up? For what?"

I don't know. But all I can think of is that time Mom made a gigantic turkey for Thanksgiving, and the recipe said to slather the whole thing, first, with butter.

We buttered that turkey up.

And then, we ate him. With organic cranberry sauce.

Gulp.

11

THIS WOULD BE the perfect time to do absolutely nothing, to dawdle endlessly or to just stare out into the abyss. Between the newfound revelations about the likely explosion on our parents' boat and the arrival of our extremely hirsute, aka hairy, Uncle Finn . . . it's been quite a day.

Frankly, I'm exhausted.

Staring up at the top of the amber-lit teepee in the middle of Henry's fortress, I can't help but wonder if this isn't all happening in some delirium I might be having. Maybe I have a fever, a hundred-and-three fever, and everything happening around me is just some fugue! My fever will break soon and all will be well. I will be back to normal and I'll look back at all of this as the ravings of a lunatic. A madman. That doesn't seem right.

Mad*woman*? Mad*girl*?

Henry seems to be taking this all quite differently, however. To wit, he actually seems more animated and excitable. Perhaps he has somehow built a contraption to suck the energy out of my veins and use it for his own mad-scientist purposes.

"Eva, do you realize what this means?"

"Which part? The explosion part or the Uncle Finn part? Either way, I'm getting confused."

"Uncle Finn!" Henry whispers. "He could help us. Don't you see? We could enlist him as an ally . . ."

"For what?"

"To uncover the mystery. Look, Eva, something is fishy here."

"*Fishy?* Are you saying that because we just got back from the marina?"

"I forgive your infantile joke. But let's weigh the evidence. Number one. There was an explosion on the boat. Very suspicious. Number two. Uncle Finn accused Uncle Claude of *buttering us up.*"

"Yes, I do admit. That was weird."

"And number three. The diorama in Uncle Claude's office building. He was really strange about it. Almost as if he were guilty of something. Not to mention how weird he was about giving us a ride to the marina . . . thereby forcing me to create an elaborate marine biology day camp ruse."

"And what a ruse it was! Well done."

"Thank you. Your praise is appreciated." Henry bows his

head. "But, again, why was Uncle Claude so strange about that condo diorama?"

"Maybe he just didn't want us sneaking around. Or breaking it."

"It was cardboard."

"Yes, but it was quite delicate." I elaborate: "Don't you remember the little fake plastic trees and miniature people everywhere? There was even a miniature dog. A schnauzer. I have to say, I really admired the attention to detail."

Henry is just about to insist on something else when we are interrupted by the sound of a hillbilly.

"You kids best start putting it all out on the table!"

Our great-great-great-great-grandfather Beaumont, the hillbilly, to be precise.

Henry and I look around the tent and suddenly, there they all are, crowded *inside* Henry's mystical teepee, the ghosts of our ancestors. It's really a little bit tight but no one seems to mind.

"Well, kids! What'dya find?" Plum leans in, fluttering her feathered Victorian fan.

"Don't leave out any details! We'll get this figgered!" Beaumont exclaims.

"Heartily, heartily." August and Sturdevant nod.

"Well." Henry looks at me, possibly wanting to make sure I, too, am witnessing our ghoulish relatives. "We believe 'Vine Thebo' actually meant 'find the boat.'"

Plum gasps. "Well, how about that!"

"Dagnabbit." Beaumont slaps his knee.

"What, what?" August and Sturdevant each raise an eyebrow.

Maxine purrs from across the teepee, "Clearly, we were all mistaken. What fools."

Henry shrugs. "Not fools, really. It's just. Well, we found the boat. And there was an—"

"Albatross!" Plum guesses.

"Alligator!" Now Beaumont.

"Otter!" Plum again.

"Aborigine!" August and Sturdevant chime in.

"Antiquated idea of the dominant paradigm?" Maxine says, rounding it out.

Henry and I look at each other.

"No, no. Not any of that," he says. The ghosts look at each other, a bit embarrassed. Henry pulls the Poseidon from its place under the blanket he's sitting on and holds it out. ". . . An explosion."

"Leaping lizards!" Beaumont jumps up.

"Oh, heavens!" Plum begins fanning herself furiously.

"Horrible. Oh, most horrible," August and Sturdevant proclaim, appalled.

"Every day, every millisecond, is an explosion, if you count the thousands and thousands of meager lives churning slowly and endlessly toward the abyss," Maxine laments.

"The point is"—I jump in—"the point is something very

odd is happening and it's becoming clear that someone wanted to get rid of our parents. On purpose. But the question is why."

"Also, as a tangential issue, would it be possible to know in advance when you ghosts plan on appearing? It's quite unsettling, the way you're just suddenly *there*. Perhaps we could make a schedule," Henry suggests.

"Oh, bless your heart." Plum beams.

"No need to worry. Just ghosts!"

"Rather." "Quite!" August and Sturdevant nod.

"One could argue we are all ghosts in some sense of the word . . ." Maxine inhales off her long cigarette lighter dramatically, the smoke billowing up through her tasseled figure.

"Dagnabbit! It's like living with the Grim Reaper!" Beaumont huffs, rolling his eyes at Maxine.

"Oh, Beaumont, she's just young!" Plum says in her defense.

"Young! My eye! She's over a hundred years old!"

"Indeed, indeed!" August and Sturdevant clink martini glasses.

"All right, listen!" Henry interrupts. "We need your assistance. We need to know the truth. Are we in danger here? In this house?"

The ghosts finally quiet down and look at each other. It seems, almost imperceptibly, that they're debating whether to tell the entire truth.

Finally, Maxine turns her head to us.

"My dears, no one in life is entirely safe."

"What do you mean?" I muster the courage to ask.

"I mean, sweet darling, the clock is ticking. On everyone."

And, in what seems like a moment of infinite sadness, the ghosts suddenly fade out into the sienna Sioux painting and the only thing left is Henry and me, standing there, wondering how long this clock will tick.

12

IF YOU EVER wanted to go to the most awkward dinner on the face of the universe, you are going to *wish* you were a part of the bit I'm about to tell you.

Dinnertime. Marisol has made snapper Veracruz with couscous and little green olives. It was always one of Dad's favorites. Terri and Claude don't care for capers.

The dynamic duo sit on opposite ends of the table, in the formal dining room, which is to say the dining room nobody ever uses except for when my mom used to employ the table as a kind of horizontal filing cabinet. Uncle Finn sits across from us. Henry and I sit side by side, elbowing each other most of the time, between giving each other furtive looks.

Marisol was unceremoniously disinvited to this dinner, as

she has been from every dinner since Terri the Terrible came to town. She seems to think Marisol should eat in her room . . . or not eat at all . . . or something.

Regardless of her dismissal of our beloved nanny (or perhaps because of it?) Terri is unusually *alive* this evening. Her face is flushed, and her eyes are a-twinkle, and when Claude offers her wine with dinner she says, "Just water."

Just. Water. It's enough to make your head spin.

"Well, you're never going to *believe* what I've been up to," Terri chirps, taking a big icy gulp from her glass. "I discovered a stable with a *roping team* just about forty-five minutes east of here, in Rancho Tierra Grande. Can you believe it?"

I can believe it, even though it's hard to understand the fascination Terri has with this . . . sport? But her mood is good, so I decide to keep her talking. "Tell me more!" I say, leaning my chin in my hand.

"Well, I'm not a beginner, of course, but boy was I rusty. I signed up for some lessons with this nice ranch hand. And then there's a spa next door, and there was kind of this package deal. It was sort of expensive, but—"

"Couldn't you be doing something more productive with your time and money?" Finn asks.

Terri frowns, confused. "What do you mean?"

"A spa? At a tourist trap? That's not real. You know what's real? The farm workers up in Castroville. I read an article about it just last week. Do you know what kind of wage they earn while *you* pay for someone to play cowboy with you?"

"Hey!" Claude shuts him down. "That's no way to speak to my girlfriend. Have a little respect."

Silence.

Terri looks, I dare say, *wounded*. I hate to admit it, but I feel for her. It's like she had a shiny red balloon, and Uncle Finn popped it.

Really the only sound you can hear is the sound of all of us eating. Henry and I, our snapper; the adults, their takeout from Gelson's supermarket hot-food counter, which was Terri's idea.

"Aren't these short ribs delicious? Mmm. They just fall off the bone. We used to have ribs like this back home. Sometimes at the rodeo. They always had the best ribs. Honey-basted. But with a little kick."

Back to another awkward silence.

Claude turns to Terri. "Hon, why don't you invite Marisol to eat with us? You girls should try to get along. Girl power!"

Uncle Finn gives Uncle Claude a withering look. "That is so insensitive of you. You are talking about grown women. Not girls. Don't infantilize them."

"Don't infantil-what? I'm just saying everyone should get along, for goodness' sake. Enough trouble in the world without making it." Claude dabs his mouth with a napkin.

"Neutrality always benefits the side of the oppressor," Finn replies.

"What? All we're doing is having our barbecue rib dinner here." He turns his chair more fully toward Finn. "You know, you've always been a nut, ever since Oberlin. Why couldn't you go to business school? Do something normal?"

"If I thought for a minute that I would have to set foot in the Wharton School of Business, I would have plunged myself into the Delaware first!"

"Delaware?! Why would you plunge yourself into Delaware?"

"The Delaware Bay, you idiot! The Atlantic Ocean feeds into Philadelphia from the Delaware Bay. How do you not know this?! You're the one who went there, oh my *God*—"

Claude scowls down at his baby backs. "Maybe I was focusing more attention on actually *attaining my degree* than flitting about between philosophy, world religions, chemistry, theater, and, my personal favorite, *semiotics*. Whatever the hell *that* is."

Finn gives Claude a sarcastic smile, turns to me, and then scruffs my hair. "Did I ever tell you about the time I got stranded with only one camel in Rajasthan?"

"Oh, here we go." Claude rolls his eyes.

"We'd trekked for hours from the Koda Village, ridden our camel through the isolated sand dunes of Khayala—"

Claude loudly scrapes his chair back and heads for the side table at the other side of the room. A gilded thing with assorted bottles and decanters, glistening under the light of the crystal chandelier.

"No amount of alcohol can cover your sins, dear brother," Finn muses.

"Sins?! What sins? You mean like actually doing something with my life?! Like not loafing around like a deranged sloth pretending to be some kind of Robinson Crusoe? Don't even try to warp these kids with your do-nothing shenanigans."

Henry and I look at each other, the weight of the room now on us.

"Fellas, cool it." Terri wipes her barbecue hands on her napkin. "You're giving me a weapons-grade headache."

"Um, I think we're going to turn in . . . right, Henry? It's been an awfully long day. Hasn't it?" Even the damask wallpaper cannot cover the sound of the seeping, entrenched resentments. I nod at Henry, trying to get us out of this completely uncomfortable situation.

"Indeed. I, too, am feeling quite fatigued. May we be excused, please?" Henry asks, always the gentleman.

"Sure, get outta here. I know I would." Terri nods.

Henry and I go to head up the stairs, when Terri stops us. "Tell Marisol . . . tell her she's welcome to some ribs if she'd like."

Finn shakes his head. "Too little too late," he mutters under his breath. We go, leaving behind a room heavy as bricks. On the landing we hear a tone we haven't heard before from Terri.

"Those kids deserve better than the two of you at each other's throats. You should be ashamed of yourselves."

I can practically feel Claude and Finn staring each other down over the centerpiece.

Henry and I share a glance. Is it possible there is another side to Terri we didn't know about? A side that might possibly have a normal, beating, cattle-roping heart?

Life is full of surprises.

13

MOST PEOPLE DON'T have a chalkboard in their room but most people aren't Henry. On the board are scribbled down a few facts:

BOAT SUNK
EXPLOSION?
NO WITNESSES
MOTIVE . . . ?
ACCIDENT . . . ?

Henry steps back from the chalkboard, gazing at the white chalk chicken scratches.

I contemplate.

"It really feels like there's something—"

But Uncle Finn comes moseying in and sees the chalkboard. "Something what?"

Henry quickly erases everything; the words disappear into little circular white clouds.

"Um, Henry and I were just making a list of things—"

"—we want to purchase in the coming year," Henry says.

Uncle Finn smiles. "Okay, little dudes, whatever. I was just coming up here to see if you guys needed anything. Maybe if you wanted to talk. Or watch a movie. Although, I think it's past your bedtime. I guess I just felt bad about all that down there at dinner. We shouldn't talk that way in front of you kiddos. It's not cool. Honestly, I'm sorry."

Henry and I don't seem to know what to say to this.

We nod. "It's okay."

"Okay, well, I just wanted you little dudes to know . . . I'm right here if you need me. *¿Comprenden?*"

"*Sí, cómo no,*" Henry replies. To which Uncle Finn looks like he has no idea what he's talking about.

"Yes, of course," I translate.

"Hey, what's that?" Finn nods in the direction of Henry's teepee.

Henry sees it first, and swoops down, throwing his little body over the statuette of Poseidon. "Something I'm working on! Something . . . nothing! Nothing really."

"Come on, kiddo. Let me see?" Finn cajoles.

Henry glances up at me. I shrug.

He hands over the hunk of metal.

"Whoa." Finn turns the statue over in his hands. He seems to understand its importance on a deep, deep level. He closes his eyes and sighs. "You miss them, I know," he says.

"Actually? You have no idea," I tell him.

Finn nods. He walks out in awkward silence. Henry and I wait for his exit. The door closes behind him.

Henry turns to me. "I think our best plan is to get a reasonable amount of sleep, wake up at dawn, analyze our current information, and plot our course of action."

"Yes. Whatever you just said, let's do that."

The house is quiet now and I am left all by my lonesome while Henry goes to brush his teeth down the hall. Outside, the moon is waning over the ocean and there's a stillness to the house, but not a calm. It's the feeling of something ready, something about to pounce. Like the moment before it rains.

I keep thinking our new best friends, the ancestor ghosts, are going to come floating in the room at any minute, arguing over each other and giving us some sort of essential clue. But tonight they are silent, waiting in the wings. Maybe they have another duty to dispatch.

Or maybe they are as confused as we are.

14

THE NEXT MORNING, the room is pitch black when we are literally rattled out of bed.

"Kids! Kiiiiiiids!"

It feels like the entire house is shaking, not unlike an earthquake, which is the logical thing to assume, as we are in California, really not that far from the San Andreas Fault, on the North American tectonic plate, which is locked in a never-ending battle with the Pacific tectonic plate.

"Wake up, you little scamps!" That's definitely Beaumont.

I am beginning to know that hillbilly voice before I see it.

And now the soothing voice of Plum, fanning herself in the corner, seems to calm the rumbling. The tumbling of the room begins to wane.

"Beaumont! Why on earth do you insist on all this ruckus!" She swats at him with her fan.

"Aw, Plum! Where's your sense of adventure? What's the point in being a ghost if you can't ruffle a few feathers?!" Beaumont winks at us, a twinkle in his eye.

Henry and I brush ourselves off and rub our eyes, recovering on the wooden floor. We stare up, in a fog, at our bickering ancestor ghosts.

"It's quite unnecessary!" Plum insists.

"Most indubitably, most indubitably." August and Sturdevant nod in agreement.

"It reminds me of the great earthquake of 1906, the devastation, the fires; the endless blaze and the indifference of humanity. How we struggle and struggle against unyielding gods, such callous, reckless power. Laughing at us."

Of course, that's Maxine, splayed out in the other corner, draped over Henry's dresser.

"Jeez, how on earth did I give rise to this one?! It's like she fell off the sad-sack wagon!" Beaumont yawps.

"Children." Plum turns to us, full of grace. "You must continue your investigation! It is your destiny."

Henry and I manage to find each other in the dark. We wouldn't admit it, but we happen to be clutching each other right now.

"But—but how?" I sputter. "I mean what should we do?"

"Return," Plum suggests.

"Return?" I rasp.

"To the boat," Plum goes on mysteriously. "You found something there once and there is more to be discovered!"

"You only know what you perceive. That is everything and nothing," Maxine purrs from the corner.

"Indeed, indeed," August and Sturdevant chime in.

"I'm sorry. I think I'm missing something—" But I'm interrupted.

"*Exactly.*" Plum nods, full of mystical meaning.

Now all the ancestor ghosts nod in dramatic agreement and slowly begin fading back into the mahogany woodwork.

"Next time, maybe not so much with the earthquakes! You know, it can be very disconcerting!" I call after them. But they are gone.

UNCLE FINN IS doing Jivamukti Yoga on the back lawn, because of course he is.

The sun rises over the house, casting amber light over the jade grass to the cliffs. It's not yet seven a.m., so even the blue-birds, flickers, and towhees are content in their slumber.

Right now Finn's legs are flung over his head like two wet noodles. This seems like the perfect time for Henry to interrupt him.

"Uncle Finn, we need to ask a favor."

Uncle Finn lurches, startled by Henry's voice, and flips over backward, turning himself into sort of a tilted pretzel in the morning light.

"Sorry. I didn't mean to scare you," Henry apologizes.

"No problem, little dudes. What's up?"

I'm still trying to stifle my giggles. I place my hand in front of my face in an attempt to hold it together. Uncle Finn is now looking up at us from *between* his spindly legs.

"Do you think you can possibly give us a ride to the marina?"

"It's important," I add, sounding official.

"Sure, you little rapscallions. You do what you need to do, and I'll commune with the sea goddess. Maybe I'll even see a pod of dolphins."

Henry and I share a quick look. *Right.* If Uncle Finn gives us a ride to the marina, we might have to take him on the boat with us. And if we take him on the boat with us, we might have to kinda sorta tell him what we're up to.

"Um. Maybe you could just give us a ride there? No need to search for dolphins or whatever. They're probably not even there, because they just like to usually hang out up above, in Marin, this time of year basically . . ." I stammer.

Henry makes a pained face. Awkward.

"Oh. Sure, dudes. No problemo." He flips over.

"Thanks, Uncle Finn. I appreciate it. Also, do you mind if we leave, like, right now, before everybody wakes up?" I ask.

"Why?"

"It's just, I wouldn't want anyone to worry about us, because, you know, sometimes if people leave early in the morning you could wonder about things like where they're going . . . do they have a secret newspaper route . . . or are they interning at a Starbucks but not wanting to say anything because that's a multinational corporation that tactically freezes out the competition, devastating all the mom-and-pop cafés and contributing to the generic social experience." I'm really going for it.

Uncle Finn just looks at me.

Henry tries to make it better. "Also, you know what they say, the early bird gets the worm!"

Finn looks at us and tilts his head. "If I didn't know any better I'd think you two little ragamuffins might be up to something . . ."

Henry and I look at each other, then back at Uncle Finn.

"Nope." I shrug. "Just perfectly normal kid stuff."

"All right then. I'll get the keys!" Finn does a kind of backflip and heads for the house.

Breakwater Cove, here we come.

16

AS WE NEAR the marina, it's clear both Henry and I are feeling guilty. Our parents drilled it into us not to be deceitful, and here we are lying all over the place like scheming banshees. The car pulls up to the fairly empty parking lot. There are a few fishermen down at the end of one dock, readying their boats, but other than that, it's pretty sparse.

I give Henry a look. I don't even have to say anything. We're both feeling it.

He shrugs.

"Um. Uncle Finn? We have something important to tell you but you have to keep it secret." I wade carefully into this crazy conversation.

"Are you looking for a lost city? That's it, isn't it? Is it the lost city of Atlantis? Or the Lost City of Zed? You found evidence, didn't you, you little tiny geniuses?"

"No. It's actually kind of more serious than that. This is kind of like . . . a thing."

"Sure. I'm sorry, I didn't mean to sound like I was diminishing your emotions," Uncle Finn says.

"No, I just. Well, we just. We need you to, uh . . . brace yourself a bit."

"Okay. I'm braced. Consider me firmly and most unflinchingly braced."

Henry and I exhale.

"All right." Henry explains: "We have reason to believe our parents' deaths may not be as simple as they seem." It comes out a bit too formal, sort of a defense.

"What? Are you serious?" Uncle Finn looks at us in disbelief.

"I know. I know it sounds strange. But there's . . ." Henry looks at me. Okay, no, he's *not* going to explain to Uncle Finn that we have been being periodically visited by ancestor ghosts for a week. That sounds nutso.

"There have just been a lot of strange things happening. Let's not get into the minor details, Henry," I add.

"Right. Right now we're just in the *investigation and proof collection* stage," Henry affirms, sounding official.

"Proof? What kind of proof? Proof of what?" Uncle Finn seems taken aback.

Maybe this wasn't such a good idea. What if he just thinks

we're psychotic and tells everyone and we get shipped off to the funny farm by those guys in white coats. Rubber Room City, population: 2.

"We think, well, maybe our parents' accident . . . wasn't an accident."

Finn gasps. He claps both hands over his mouth. He appears, to be honest, a bit green.

After a few moments he asks, "Not an accident? But why? How? Who could—"

"Honestly, we're working on that part." I turn to Henry for an assist.

"We're still gathering evidence."

Uncle Finn thinks for a moment. "Are you kids serious?"

"Pretty serious." I nod. "More serious than not."

"Sixty, maybe sixty-two percent serious," Henry guesses.

Finn looks at us, our two little heads looking up at him, framed by the bright blue sky. We are two lost puppies in a storm. He sighs.

"Okay, little dudes. Whatever you need. But I'm really hoping this is all a big mix-up, 'cause otherwise it's just . . . too much of a bummer."

I nod. That is one way to put it.

Should we touch on the ghost part now? It occurs to me that if anyone would believe us about these ghosts, it would be Uncle Finn.

"Hey, um, did you *feel* anything last night?" I ask him. "Like a tremor, or a quaking of some sort?"

Henry elbows me, shaking his head. Clearly he doesn't want me to go any further into it.

"Nope. Why, was there an earthquake and I missed it? Figures. I sleep like the dead. No offense. I snored right through a 6.0 in Bangladesh once. If you can believe it."

He didn't feel it. So, for now, I guess we'll just stick to a simple fact-finding expedition on the boat.

Easy breezy. You know. Unless there's a murderer running loose.

17

THERE'S THE *IDEA* of the thing we're doing and then there's the *actual* thing we're doing. Intellectually, it's easy to think about it, plot, strategize. But if I let myself fall off that particular one-foot-in-front-of-the-other, check-all-the-boxes-in-the-to-do-list life raft . . . then the gut-churning reality of actually going back out to sea, to hover above the spot where our parents perished . . . that's sort of where I start to fall apart.

I have to brace myself against it.

I just need to keep the fact-finding part of this mission up high in the uppermost reaches of my cranium, or there's no way I can keep this up. If I let this dark matter creep down from the lizard part of my brain, down my neck and chest, into my heart, there is the very real possibility that I might just break down.

My knees might buckle and the air just might start coming in and out in gasps.

So this must continue to stay a strictly intellectual operation.

It's official: I'm now living exactly where Henry lives. Smack dab in the middle of my brain. Actually, the middle of the left side. The logical part. The rational one. The analytical one. The other side? The right side? The one that processes art and sadness and emotions? Well, I am sending that one to take a powder for the day. Bye, right side. See you in the funny pages.

This marina, as you know, is in Monterey Bay. If you ever want to visit, there's an uber-cool aquarium right on top of the rock cliffs where you can look down and see an actual real tide pool, attached to the ocean and everything. It's early morning now, so it's not open, but I make a vow to check it out on our way back. My mom used to take us there every month, so going there is kind of like being with . . .

Stop, right brain! Go away!

The good news is our favorite sea captain, Wayne from the land Down Under, is setting up the rigging at the end of the dock. I am glad he has not been overtaken by hobbits.

"Wayne! Hey, Wayne! Remember us?!"

He looks up from his sailor knot. "Well, didn't expect to see you young 'uns back so soon! Who's this, then?"

We introduce him to Uncle Finn and he gives him a hearty handshake.

"Ah, Kiwi?" Finn guesses.

"Right you are. Good ear." Wayne smiles, looking back at us.

"So, um. Do you think you would mind taking us out again?" I ask.

"We'll pay you for your trouble," Uncle Finn offers.

"Aw, no. No trouble for these kids, then." He nods at us kindly. "Knew their folks. Good people."

"Too good," Finn replies in a near whisper.

I would hug him, but *logical brain* time.

The dock is starting to hum with activity, as bit by bit more sailors and fishermen come out to greet the day, over the docks. By the time we get out past the breakwater, I can even see a tour group arriving, one by one laughing and boarding a larger boat, *"Monterey Jitney"* written across the bow. Lots of men in khaki shorts and women in sun hats. They look around, expectantly, excited for a day out at sea. I want to be excited with them.

As we cruise out, Uncle Finn takes in the view, the little Craftsman homes getting smaller and smaller until they look like tiny dollhouses, placed pristinely on the hills.

The last of the golden light burns off into the pale blue sky above, fading in, devoid of clouds or even a thought of a cloud. The waters are calm today, hardly even any whitecaps, just deep, dark indigo. I'm hoping for a whale sighting, as we are in the middle of the humpback migration period, but who knows.

"We're heading out from Point Lobos, where the last signal was logged," Henry explains to Uncle Finn.

Wayne looks back at Finn and me, standing on the starboard side, peering out.

"You might as well have a seat, then. This should take a while."

Henry nods, concurring.

Gazing back at the wake of the boat, I try not to think about what could have happened here. I try to just get lost in the triangle of whitewash behind the boat, kicked up by the motor, the light reflected off the water, and the big blue sea. There's a lullaby here, a calming, as if the ocean itself is rocking me, singing a song about eternity and what was here before and what will be here after.

Uncle Finn is silent, too, taking it in. Not even a word.

None of us say *the* word. Explosion. That's a word we keep down deep, deeper than the silt and Dungeness below.

I keep my eyes out for some harbor seals, sea otters, or maybe a pod of bottlenose dolphins. Sometimes they'll come and play in the wake, or race along near the front of the boat at lightning speed, little gray-and-white torpedoes in the water. Every once in a while they'll pop out of the water, flying and surfing. I swear, you can almost see them smile when they jump. They're curious, so sometimes they just swim by to investigate, see what's shaking. Once you see them spiraling and frolicking in the waves, you'll never again want to see them anywhere but there, out in the water, free, in the great wide ocean.

If I see them today, I will join them. I'll throw myself into the current and race out to sea with my new pod of bottleneck dolphins who will raise me up as one of their own. Then, when you come out past the breakwater, you will see *me* torpedo through the wake of the boat; you'll think you recognize me but I'll be gone before you know it, off with my new pod to adventures off the coast of Southern climes, past Catalina, Ensenada, and down to La Paz.

No one will find me there.

18

THE SKY IS turning marble blue before we reach the coordinates. The wind is sending a chill down over the bow of the boat.

I'm not sure what I expect to find here. What we were supposedly sent back for. To revisit.

Maybe more evidence? Maybe something we missed?

Neither Henry nor I mention that we are here on the advice of a gaggle of ghosts.

"There! There it is." Henry and Wayne focus on the screen. This is it. The exact spot where we realized there had been an explosion. The exact spot where we were relieved of any semblance of normalcy in our lives. This so-called accident.

But it could have been an accident.

Why *couldn't* it have been? That's really the issue. Just because there was an explosion doesn't necessarily mean there was anything purposeful or nefarious, right?

"I don't know what we're looking for." It comes out like a plea.

Wayne looks up at me from the bow, concerned.

Uncle Finn gently places his hand on my shoulder. "Maybe we ought to sit back a bit, what do you say? Look, it's a beautiful day out, look at that light on the water. Breathtaking."

He walks me gently aft, back to the stern.

I know Henry. He'll keep it logical. He'll keep this as a scientific experiment, square on the left side of his brain, for as long as he can. Maybe forever.

But Uncle Finn is right, taking me away from that screen. Here, looking out the port side, back at the distant cliffs with the sun coming down, painting their sides into gold, maybe I don't want to know any more about what happened. Maybe I don't want to know anything again.

Uncle Finn puts his coat around me.

"You have to stay ahead of the cold. If your bones get cold out here, it'll be too late. You'll never warm up."

He's right about that. This kind of wet cold, over the ocean current, if it gets under your skin you'll be cold for months. Once my mom made me take a two-hour steaming-hot bath to get the ocean air out of my skeleton.

No! Left brain, stop! Don't think about that right now. Don't ever think about that again.

Uncle Finn puts a delicate arm around me while Henry, now apparently Captain Wayne's adopted nephew, conjectures.

"Look! Look, Eva!" Finn leaps up.

He points out over the bow, starboard, out to sea. There, about one hundred feet away, I see it. A humpback whale migrating south. Sometimes if you see one, you'll see the whole family, but this one appears solo. Probably a male.

He's not breaching or doing anything showy, he's just quietly glissading parallel to us. Stealth.

"Henry!"

Henry and Captain Wayne both come aft to see the whale.

We all stand in silence, taking in this majestic creature, pondering him as he ponders us.

This is the best part.

Just as the whale is gliding past us, he rolls slightly, turning his colossal body so his eye can see us. His giant eye looks almost human in shape, and even cognizant, peering directly at us, while his enormous body angles just out of the water.

A moment.

And then down again, plunging under the water and then gone.

We all look at each other, speechless.

19

WHEN THE WHALE dives back down under the deep sapphire sea, there's a stillness. A hush of disappointment. A kind of feeling like we'd just seen some kind of mystical, eternal, transcendent creature and now the only thing left was the dreary rest of it. The day-to-day. A life measured out in coffee spoons.

And then it hits me.

We are not looking for something that is.

We are looking for something that isn't.

"Henry!"

He glances back at me from the stern.

"I know what it is! I know what we missed!"

Henry comes aft toward me, and Uncle Finn shuffles out

of the way, wanting to give us privacy. He and Captain Wayne share a look.

"What, Eva? What is it?"

"It's not what *we're* missing," I tell him. "It's what *is* missing."

Henry's face scrunches in an attempt to understand.

"Captain Wayne," I call, "turn the boat around. It's time to go back."

20

THE BOAT IS speeding back through the swells toward the dock, Captain Wayne and Uncle Finn at the helm, Henry and me aft, huddled in toward each other, talking in hushed tones, the steady drone of the motor almost drowning us out.

"Do you remember the one thing Mom was OCD about?" I ask.

Henry shakes his head. "Honestly, no."

"Think about it. What was the one thing Mom would get truly bent out of shape about? Every single time we went on the boat . . . ?"

"Well . . . she was always a bit paranoid . . . about safety."

"Exactly."

Henry looks back at the wake, an ivory froth triangle

billowing out from behind, slicing the sea into pieces.

"The life vests!" he realizes.

"Bingo."

Now it's like watching a maze form, setting itself up in the perimeter of his mind.

"Mom would never have left the dock without the life vests," I go on. "Remember? She even refused to keep them in the hold so they'd be 'readily accessible' or whatever."

"That's true," Henry concurs.

"So, think about it. Look back and think about every shot on the news of every plane crash or boat accident . . . What do you always see, floating around everywhere on the top of the waves . . . ?"

A moment while the maze falls into place.

"The life vests," Henry realizes.

"Right. And Mom insisted on keeping them right up on deck, always, at all times, no exceptions. So . . . they would have floated up. Someone would have *found them*."

"Right. And if they never floated up out of the water, which they would have . . . they must not have been on the boat."

It hits us at the same time.

"Someone must have taken them off the boat," I say.

For the first time, the very first time . . . that implies *purpose*. Before, we could have, if we wanted to, believed that everything was a mishap. The explosion was some kind of accident. A misfortune. A terrible twist of fate, but only that. Nothing planned. Nothing nefarious.

But now, considering the idea that there were no life vests on board, taking into account our mother's obsessive-compulsive insistence on having them within arm's reach at all times, it's clear.

Someone purposefully took the life vests off the boat.

"Whoever took them off. That's our guy," I whisper.

"Or girl," Henry offers.

Maybe in all this discovery we were hoping to be proven wrong. Or somehow let off the hook. But this is the opposite of being let off the hook. Now there is proof. Intent. Now there is something malicious where before there was just a bunch of clues and guesswork and conjecture. Now there is collusion.

"Well, looks like we made good time, then." Captain Wayne guides the boat toward the marina, giving us a reassuring smile.

"Thanks for helping us, Captain Wayne. We really can't thank you enough. Right, Henry?" Henry nods and the two of us step forward, readying ourselves to dock.

"No kidding! Wow. Mother Nature is a beauty. This has been quite an adventure, little dudes." Uncle Finn smiles, helping us off the boat.

Standing on the dock, looking back at Captain Wayne as he rearranges the rigging, it comes to me.

"So, um. Captain Wayne, have you seen any life vests around? Like extra ones . . . anywhere?"

"Let me see . . ." He ponders it, leaning over to tighten a sailor knot to the cleat. "Nope. Not that I can think of, no."

"Anything? Like in the past few months? Just sort of lying

around?" Henry continues.

"If you kiddos need some life vests, I can buy you some. No problem. I'm sure they sell them nearby," Uncle Finn offers.

"No, it's not that," Henry tells him.

"Sorry, kids." Wayne shakes his head, his reddish-blond hair turning bronze in the sun.

Henry, Uncle Finn, and I make our way back up the dock. It's about fifty feet of creaky, gray, weathered boards, the smell of fish coming off the water.

We're just about near the parking lot when we hear it.

"Hang on, kids!" Wayne comes walking up, winded. "I just remembered—every once in a while one of these richy-rich types comes down from San Francisco, then rents a yacht and doesn't know a thing about safety first. You know, pretty girls in heels and all that. They think they're in a hip-hop video. Well, they never have the proper amount of life jackets for their numbers, so they end up just buying them here, else they can't go out, against harbor rules, you know. So they just buy them up and leave them here. Truly wasteful, if you ask me. You know how they are up there. Lavish. New money. We usually just throw the extras up in the old boathouse over there . . ."

He gestures to the slate-blue-and-white little wooden boathouse at the end of the pier, sitting over the water with one lone orange life preserver attached to the side.

"It's chock-full of them, actually. Floor to ceiling. Just take your pick. Be warned, though. Some of them might have some vomit on them, and the like. You know, these city folks get on the boat and get seasick. Landlubbers."

Henry and I nod and take off toward the boathouse.

We throw open the door.

It's a solid wall of orange life jackets. Some of them tumble down in a mini avalanche. We jump back, and they settle on the dock around our feet.

Henry turns to our uncle. "Uncle Finn, not to be rude, but you might want to make yourself comfortable. This is going to take a while."

21

THE INSIDE OF the boathouse smells like a combination of mold, salt, fish, and a bit of something chemical, I'm assuming from the life jackets. Captain Wayne was right, this place is *packed*.

I can't help but think someone else could put these to better use, halfway across the world somewhere.

"What, exactly, are we looking for, little dudes?" Uncle Finn follows us in. Henry is already picking up life jacket after life jacket, inspecting, scrutinizing, throwing to the side.

"We should send some of these to those in need," I suggest, inspecting on my own. "This seems like a waste."

"Agreed. Uncle Finn, you really don't have to help us. Just take a seat. This is really just too tedious," Henry says.

"Well, I can help. I'd like to, if you'd let me," he offers. "Just tell me what I'm looking for."

"Honestly, Uncle Finn, even I'm not sure what *I'm* looking for," I tell him.

"How many of these babies do you think are in here, anyway? One hundred? Two hundred?" Uncle Finn looks around at the mass of orange flotation devices.

"I'm not sure, some of them seem really old, actually," I say, picking up a life jacket that looks like it might have come off the *Titanic*. I resist the urge to sing the theme song from the movie. *Not now, Eva.* "Seems like they've been chucking them in here for decades."

Uncle Finn stares out at the waves through the boathouse's tiny window. He seems lost in thought. We give him his moment.

Meanwhile, Henry and I stay hard at work. We inspect each one of the life vests.

After about an hour, I'm beginning to think it's obvious that this is an exercise in futility. I mean, if someone *did* take the life vests off Mom's boat, which I am one hundred percent convinced is true, they could now be anywhere. In Timbuktu. In Guadalajara. Even (shudder) in Los Angeles. They could have been thrown in the trash, or sent to Kalamazoo.

"Henry, do we really think the life vests are here? Why would they be?"

"Because this is the most logical place for them." Henry doesn't even look up from his investigating.

"How do you figure?" I ask.

"Well, Eva, think about it like this. Let's say you were going to steal the life jackets off a boat for nefarious reasons."

"Yes?"

"Now, anywhere you would take those life jackets would point to you. Even if you left them in a Dumpster at the gas station in Poughkeepsie for instance."

"O-kaaay . . ."

"All of a sudden, there would most probably be video of you leaving said life jackets in a random Dumpster. Very suspicious," Henry continues. "No way to explain it away."

"True."

"However, if you were smart, which let's assume this person or persons is . . . you would not take the life jackets anywhere out of this exact marina. Thereby leaving no trace, no path, no clues, no bread crumbs, et cetera et cetera et cetera."

"Maybe." I weigh it.

"And . . . if you couldn't take the life jackets out of the marina, where would be the perfect place for you to leave them where no one would ever, ever find them?"

"Um."

"Possibly with hundreds of other life jackets? In a place no one seems to have looked in, what did you call it, decades?"

"Right," I admit. "You would leave them here. In the great life jacket depository of Monterey Bay."

"Exactly," Henry gloats. "And eureka!" He holds up a small-ish life jacket and I immediately know, for the zillionth time in my life, that my brother is a super genius.

There, in his pale little hands, hangs an orange life jacket, built small-scale for a child, with the weight limit "90 lbs." stamped on the side. But that's not the important part. The important part is . . . off to the lower right-hand side of the jacket, just below the white plastic belt, in scraggly black pen . . . are three games of ticktacktoe, scrawled on the side. And a happy face where I had declared myself the winner. When I was six.

"Bingo."

22

"I'M GOING TO assume that's what you were looking for?"
Uncle Finn asks, picking himself up from the floor and dusting
off his pants.

"I think so." I hope so, at least.

Henry and I share a look. Whatever it is or whoever it is,
we're getting closer. Clearly, whoever got rid of the life jackets
had no idea that at one point, years ago, two innocent little
scamps had been playing ticktacktoe on one of those very life
jackets, only to get chastised by their mother. And clearly, they
didn't realize that would matter.

But even so, we're still no closer to figuring out *who* that
person is.

"Interesting." Henry notices the little life vest seems to be tethered to three other life vests. I recognize them. Mama bear. Daddy bear. Me bear. Don't think about that, Eva. Thinking cap on. Heart off.

"Okay, good. I don't know about you, little dudes, but I am ready to get out of this musty old boathouse." Uncle Finn yanks the life vests farther from the pile and *ting*. There is the unmistakable sound of something metal hitting the floor. "What's that?"

He stops on a dime. Looks down.

"Did you guys drop this?" Uncle Finn picks something up off the ground, beneath Henry's feet.

"Drop what?" I ask.

Henry leans in, squinting. "It looks like an old-fashioned key."

The top of the key is an intricate fleur-de-lis in bronze; the bottom is shaped like an L, with little notches in it. It almost looks like something off a pirate ship or a Victorian steam train. The kind of thing Sherlock Holmes and Watson would spend an afternoon musing about, over tea or crumpets or popovers or whatever happens over there.

"It definitely looks vintage," I say, inspecting the detail.

"Is it yours?" Uncle Finn looks up at us.

Henry and I meet eyes.

"Definitely not."

23

"OKAY, SO, KIDS? I'm officially confused," Uncle Finn admits, driving us back home along the Pacific Coast Highway, the ocean off to our right side, down the treacherous cliff. This part of the road swirls up and down, on the side of the mountains. There are railings here and there, but definitely not as many as you would need to keep from flying off the precipice into the abyss. Perilous.

"Let's see. How do I explain it?" I look to Henry for an assist. But he's a lost cause, gazing out over the sea, the sun just about to sink down into the other side of the world. A golden slit of light before the dark takes over.

"Okay, well. Here goes. We have . . . as we stated earlier . . . through various means . . . come to realize . . . that our parents' deaths were not accidental. That there was . . . an explosion."

Uncle Finn keeps his eyes on the serpentine road. "Wait. Seriously?"

"Yes, seriously. And not only that but . . . we have reason to believe it was a quite purposeful explosion." I'm trying my very best not to sound looney tunes. "Meant to sink the boat. And our parents."

Henry is still offering zero help, entranced by the blazing sunset.

"And whoever did it, took out the life jackets. Purposefully," I go on.

"So that they would die," Henry says blankly.

"Henry!" I look over at him, concerned. Then back at Uncle Finn. "So that . . . whoever was on board would not survive."

"But that's horrible! Are you sure about this? This seems like . . . I dunno . . . it seems kinda like a stretch. Like something out of a Hitchcock film or something," Uncle Finn says.

"I know. Look. We know it seems weird. But something is definitely wrong," I say. "There is literally *no other explanation* for why these life jackets would be in the boathouse. Our parents would never, *ever* have taken them off the boat."

"'Something is rotten in the state of Denmark.'" Henry stares out over the ocean, surveying the waves and the depths below.

"That's Shakespeare," I add.

Uncle Finn seems unable or unwilling to process this information. "Listen, you kids are super smart, for sure, no question. But do you think this might just be a little, teeny-tiny, maybe, exaggerated? I'm not questioning the validity of your assumptions, but, just to play devil's advocate here for a second, doesn't this all seem a teeny bit, I dunno, dramatic?"

All of a sudden, I am questioning myself. We haven't even told him yet about the recurrent spectral visitations. Jeez.

"Uncle Finn, may I see that key again?" Henry interrupts from the back, as if abruptly remembering something.

"Sure, little fella." Uncle Finn hands him the key over the back seat, eyes still fixed on the road. "You found an old, ornate key. I suppose that's gonna be a big part of the mystery, too, right?" He lets out a small chuckle, more affectionate than mocking.

I take this in. My spider-sense is telling me clearly that Uncle Finn thinks we're just two delusional little kids with no idea, grasping at straws in the wake of this terrible tragedy, just trying to find *meaning*. I'm beginning to understand why Henry didn't want to go to any adults on this particular case—our case—sooner.

"Maybe. It's possible it's just some dumb key." I shrug. An attempt at reverse psychology.

"Or it's possible it's everything," Henry proclaims matter-of-factly from the back seat. There's a kind of confidence to it as if he knows something we don't. Almost a smirk embedded in his words.

Uncle Finn and I share a look.

"You never know," Henry adds. And now he starts to whistle nonchalantly.

The whistle gives it away.

24

WHEN WE GET back to the house, Henry immediately cata-
pults out the back of the car, not even bothering to wait until
it is fully stopped. Uncle Finn and I gawk after him as he tears
up the driveway, kicking up dust all the way back up the path,
barreling through the front door.

Inside, the house is quiet, with not a single light on. Unusual
for this time of the evening. Normally, this time of night the
kitchen is lit up like Grand Central Station, with Marisol listening to NPR and chopping up vegetables in her floral-printed
apron from Anthropologie. She, my mom, and my dad all got
matching ones. I know, kind of goofy. But right now there is no
goofiness to be had. The house is abandoned, none of the sweet
smells and sights of home and hearth.

"Henry? Henry?!! Where are you?!" I call up to him from the landing, following the sound of his footsteps on the floorboards above.

Uncle Finn lags behind, taking his time over the clover-and-cobblestone path up the driveway. However, inside, upstairs, there's an urgency, a whirling tornado of activity I can hear clattering and clanking from the entry down below.

"Eva! I know what this is, I'm sure of it!"

Henry's voice echoes downstairs over the landing. I race up the stairs and down the hall to where I find him, in Claude's room, rifling through drawers and wardrobes and bureaus.

"Henry, what are you doing?! You're making a mess. We're going to have to clean this whole thing up!" This feels like a violation.

"Eva, it's here. I know it's here."

"I think maybe you should sit down, Henry. I mean, it's been a big day. What with the life jackets and everything. Maybe you should have a drink of water." I'm beginning to be concerned. Henry has a tendency to get a bit obsessed, as evidenced by his . . . everything.

"Don't you see, Eva?! It's all coming together. The whole thing!"

"What whole thing? Henry, what are you talking about? Look, I really think we should just sit down for a second. Maybe do some deep-breathing exercises."

Anybody else would be aghast. Henry is like a hurricane blasting his way through the entire room, turning it upside down.

Uncle Finn saunters in, backpack over his shoulder, a twisted smirk on his face. "Whoa, so *this* is the viper's nest?"

Strong words, I think. "You and Uncle Claude really don't care for each other, do you?"

Finn begins to snoop right along with Henry, lifting a folded sweater here, piece of paper there.

"Let's just say we have—different approaches to life." He shakes his head. "I guess we've done pretty terrible things to each other over the years, but I've traveled this world. Gained some perspective." He pauses. "Some people, no matter how long they live, no matter how much they have, they just never see the light."

Wow. Finn thinks Claude is even more terrible than we do.

Crash! Henry is essentially terrorizing every nook, cranny, and millimeter of poor Uncle Claude's bedroom. Ugh. This is going to be a nightmare to clean up.

He has now been swallowed up by the walk-in closet. Tennis rackets, shoe boxes, old weathered hats are being spewed out mad-dash from inside.

"Henry. This is enough! You're acting crazy!"

"Crazy like a fox!" Henry shouts back.

I lean into the closet. "What does that even mean? Henry, I really think we should—"

"Um, guys?"

It's Finn, and there's a tone in his voice I haven't heard before. He's wandered over to a corner of the room with an old-timey armoire. He has one of the drawers open and is staring at whatever is inside.

Henry peeks out of the closet and makes a beeline to the mahogany armoire.

He gazes in and gasps. Then he looks up at me, his face pale and flushed.

He reaches into the drawer. Takes hold of something. Then he is presenting me with it, offering it up.

I look down and see, there in his hands, a miniature wooden chest with a flourish on the lid.

"What? Henry, I don't get it."

"Look, Eva. The design."

Then it hits me, this petite wooden box.

Has the same design on it as the key. The key from the boat-house. The old-fashioned, intricate, vintage-looking key.

Henry fishes the key from his pocket. There is no doubt. The patterns are identical.

I walk forward, staring down at the key and the lock. The antique key now in the lock of the tiny wooden box. Henry stands there, his chest moving up and down, out of breath. The small-scale wooden box held up in his hands like the slabs of the Ten Commandments. The hair at his temples slightly damp from sweat. He looks up at me.

"It was Claude. He's the one. He killed our parents."

PART THREE

1

FOR NO APPARENT reason, I keep thinking about the encounter with the humpback whale. Whatever that was, that moment in the ocean, what it felt like . . . was a blessing. There was something about the whale, his expression, the purposeful-ness of it all, of how he rolled sideways and peered directly at us, that felt meant for only the two of us. Maybe to the whale, there was something soft about the two little forms on the white floating object. The smaller ones. Tender. The way we'd see a deer and his two yearlings. The way we'd want to take care of, want to protect the two baby deer. That's what it felt like. As if the whale wanted to protect us.

And yes, I may be imagining it. But Henry? Henry doesn't really just make stuff up out of the blue. It's not his style. He's very proud of his use of the scientific method and it shows with all his tinkering, experimenting, and inventions. Everything is trial and error. Surmise and experiment. Hypothesize and test.

Back here, in the safe Sioux embrace of Henry's teepee, there is room for contemplation. Room to take a breath.

"I feel like that whale came up to our boat for a reason. Like he was drawn to us," I suggest.

"I suppose it's possible," Henry replies, unmoved.

"Didn't it feel like that to you? Like the whale wanted to protect us?"

"Potentially."

"I'm not crazy, right? You felt something weird, didn't you?" I'm not sure why this matters to me quite so much, in the general context of our recent discovery. It's almost like I'm trying to trick myself. To steer the subject away from the obvious. To stall.

"It's a possibility. But there's also the possibility that we're projecting our anthropomorphic ideals onto a marine mammal."

I look into the light of the buckskin lamp, the shadows waving up, dancing.

"Maybe."

Uncle Finn is somewhere downstairs, probably rummaging through the kitchen cupboards for something to eat. It's strange that Marisol isn't back yet. But everything is abnormal these days. Just add it to the weird pile.

"We should focus on the matter at hand." Henry steers me back.

"You mean . . . Uncle Claude?"

"I don't think we should call him that."

"How about *he-who-shall-remain-nameless*?"

"Yes, that'll do."

Henry hunches over, the two of us under our respective plain hand-loomed striped blankets. "The question is . . . now that we know. What do we do?"

"But . . . *do* we know, Henry? I mean, do we really know?"

"Eva, you saw what was in that box."

Now that is true. Other than the absurd fact that the antique key we found in the boathouse *fit* that small wooden box, what was in the box was even more incriminating. Devastating, even.

"You have to admit, the evidence is overwhelming."

Again, true. The evidence from the wooden box does not look good for Uncle Claude. Here is what we found: a topographical map of our property, a copy of the deed to our house, a copy of our grandparents' will, and a map of the Monterey marina with the location of our mother's boat circled . . . there was also, indeed most devastatingly, a list of ingredients one would need to cause a not-insignificant explosion, along with a step-by-step guide to create said explosion. The kind of explosion that would, for instance, sink a small boat.

"But why would he keep all of this? That's what I want to know. Why would anyone keep such damning evidence around?" I ask.

"Maybe as a kind of a trophy. Or . . . maybe he wanted to reuse it. Maybe he wasn't done."

We let that sink in. Ominous. What would it mean for Uncle Claude not to be done? What else would there be to do? To destroy?

"Wait. Are we in danger?" I whisper.

"I think it's safe to assume everything isn't one hundred percent fine in our current situation," Henry replies.

"But what would be the point? I mean, of doing anything to . . . us?"

Henry shrugs. "Who knows? But one does have to assume that if a person is capable of . . . such things . . . then they are also capable of repeating the act."

He doesn't want to say it. He doesn't want to say "capable of killing." Those words can't be spoken out loud.

"Marisol is here!" I bleat. "Marisol would never let anything happen to us!"

Henry nods. "True, but Eva? Eva, we have to do something. The time for contemplation is over."

"What do you mean? Like do what?" I ask.

"I'm not sure." He thinks. "Should we seek revenge?"

I contemplate the flickering amber coming up through the buckskin lamp.

"You mean, like . . . an eye for an eye? No way."

"Eva Millicent Billings, our parents are dead. Because of him. Because of Uncle . . . he-who-shall-remain-nameless."

"Henry Alexander Billings, I'm aware of that. I couldn't be

more aware of that. But revenge? Mom and Dad would definitely never, ever, ever, never want that. Not in a million years."

We each stare ahead, imagining what our parents would want.

My dad wouldn't even kill a spider. I'm serious. Mom would be screaming her head off because there would be a brown recluse or a black widow or a brown widow in the bathtub. Dad would just go to the kitchen, grab a glass, go trap the spider, slide a plate under the glass, and walk said terrifying spider calmly to the backyard, where he'd set it free. And every time, like clockwork, Mom would say, "You'd better wash that glass like a hundred times. And the plate, too." He'd nod and go back to his office, winking at us on his way.

"I think it's safe to assume that if Dad wouldn't even kill a spider, he wouldn't want us to kill his brother." Henry reads my thoughts.

"Not to mention the fact that we'd go to jail. *Jail*, Henry. Do you think either of us would do very well in jail?"

"Technically, we'd go to juvenile detention," he notes.

"Technically, we'd get our butts kicked every single day. And you know it. Although, you might have an out by doing the warden's taxes, like in *The Shawshank Redemption*," I reason.

"That doesn't sound very appealing."

We adjust our respective blankets.

"Well, we have to do *something*. Don't you think?" Henry asks.

"Yes, but the question is . . . what is that something? We're basically encountering pure evil for the first time in our lives, so, excuse me if I'm not brimming with ideas."

"I wonder if it is pure evil? Perhaps it's just overwhelming greed. Without Dad around, we will inherit the house and, more important, the land. But Claude is our legal guardian; that puts him in the proverbial driver's seat."

I gasp. "Henry! The model in his office!"

"The condos!" Henry almost laughs. "He can build his hideous condos, sell them for a fortune, and laugh all the way to the bank."

"Clearly, all he cares about is money. We've seen that since he got here." I swallow the sour taste in the back of my throat. "Uncle Finn was right. He *is* a capitalist vulture. But we can't kill him! We're just kids! And if there is a hell, I do not want to go there."

"Well, maybe you just sleep. You die, you sleep. End of story." Henry shrugs.

"Or . . . maybe you wake up in an unspeakable place that we can't even imagine but it's eternal and full of monsters that bite you all day. With fangs," I add.

"'Ay, there's the rub,'" Henry quotes. "'For in that sleep of death what dreams will come?'"

"'Thus conscience doth make cowards of us all.'" I can quote *Hamlet*, too.

Are we cowards?

We look at each other, a moment of contemplating vengeance.

Henry exhales. "You're right. Our parents wouldn't want us to seek revenge. They wouldn't. They've always taught us to turn the other cheek."

"Exactly. Remember Mom used to say, 'Forgiveness is a gift to the giver.'"

"Yes. Although I'm still not sure I understand what she meant." He thinks. "All right, so revenge is out. But how about justice?"

"Justice. Like jail, right? Like we prove he's guilty and then let the courts decide. Or the jury. Or the judge. Or whatever," I ramble.

"Precisely. Due process. Truth. Justice. That's the right thing to do. The noble thing," Henry says, more to himself.

"Maybe that was what the whale was for."

"What?"

I ponder this. "Maybe the whale was, like, coming to tell us that the universe is an amazing place and we shouldn't do bad things, out of respect for the beauty of the world."

"An interesting hypothesis, Eva. It could also be that we just saw a whale."

Downstairs the front door slams shut and Terri's laughter echoes up through the stairwell.

Henry and I lock eyes.

"What do we do?" I whisper.

"We have to pretend we don't know anything. Play dumb."

But their footsteps are getting louder and louder, through the entry, up the stairs, down the hall. Toward us.

We sit frozen in the teepee, eyes locked.

Marisol will be back soon, I tell myself, repeating it like a mantra. *Marisol will be back soon. Marisol will be back soon!*

The door to the room opens and now the footsteps are coming closer, across the floor and over to us.

The looming shadow of Uncle Claude hovers above the teepee, menacing.

"Kids?"

He opens the front, now framed in a tall triangle outside our teepee.

"I want you to know. I just dropped Marisol at the train station. She won't be coming back for a while."

2

TERRI THE TERRIBLE lurks at the heels of Claude. Behind them, as now the two of them are framed in the teepee like Union invaders from the East, Uncle Finn's footsteps echo across the room.

"Hey, dudes. What's up?"

Henry and I both chime in, simultaneously, "They kicked out Marisol!"

Uncle Claude bumbles to the side. "Now hold on there, kids, no one said anything about kicking out. She got an email. Her mother was sick!"

"*Sure* she was." Henry rolls his eyes.

"No, really." Terri steps up next to Claude, defending him. "She told us her mother down in Guatemala was sick and she had to go be with her. Just in case. You know . . ."

Terri gives us a meaningful tilt of the head.

"Just in case her mother *died*," Claude blurts out. Always subtle. "I know this is a terrible shock, and awful timing. I'm so sorry, but—"

Uncle Finn weaves through them next to us, into the inner sanctum of the teepee. "Sorry, brother. Marisol would have said something to these guys before she left. She loves them like their own mother."

Henry and I share a glance; truer words have never been spoken.

Now Uncle Claude and Terri step into the teepee, which seems like a violation. "Look! I don't care what you think!"

Henry stops them. "Please do not enter my teepee. It's sacred space."

"Yes, it's sacred space. Given to Henry by Tahoma 'Blue Earth' Mankoto of the Lakota tribe of Hunkpapa, as a gift due to our father's environmental work in Standing Rock. You are not welcome here. You are not allowed. You have to be invited," I inform them.

Uncle Claude stops, schooled. Terri bumps into him. The two of them turn to leave, embarrassed.

"Go back and get Marisol! These kids need her!" Uncle Finn adds, emboldened by this tiny victory.

Uncle Claude turns back to him, red in the face. "I have a better idea! Why don't *you* pack your bags and get out of here! Right now! Tonight!"

It's more of a roar than a voice. The floorboards underneath shake and there is an abrupt silence. Even the rafters are listening.

"Is that a threat?" Uncle Finn says under his breath.

"You bet it's a threat! Get out of here, Finn! Run off to Bangladesh! Or Tahiti! Or Cairo! Go climb the pyramids! Sing with the fishes or whatever it is you people do!" Claude bellows.

"*You people?*" Finn seethes with anger. "What is *that* supposed to mean?"

Claude exhales through his nostrils, like a bull about to charge. "Our brother did not want you here. *I* do not want you here. So get. Out."

Henry and I both look up at Uncle Finn, praying he won't actually leave us. If he leaves, with Marisol gone, it's just the two of us kids stuck here with Terri the Terrible and Uncle Claude the . . . the murderer.

Terri pulls out her phone. "Should I call the police and inform them we have a trespasser?"

"I guess I can't force you to let me stay." Uncle Finn sighs.

Henry and I look up at Uncle Finn, helpless.

"Uncle Finn, you can't go. Please don't go," I plead.

"Please." Henry steps forward.

"Aw, little dudes. I sure wish I could stay, but sometimes a total jerk-face is just a total jerk-face, and that is all they are and all they will ever be no matter how much money they have or what kind of capitalist swine they turn out to be!" His face turns red at the end of that sentiment, and there's a stunned silence all around.

Uncle Claude clears his throat.

"I'm so sorry." Finn forces a smile. "I wish there was something else I could do . . ."

But he's right. There's nothing he can do. Nothing we can do.

"There's a little inn down the way. Pretty good breakfast. It's, like, a ten-minute walk. That's where I'll be . . . *if you need me.*" He says that last bit locking gazes with first me, then Henry.

Then Uncle Finn bows his head and slinks out. Just like that, our last remaining ally slips past us, past Uncle Claude and Terri the Terrible, out of the room and, tonight, out of our lives.

Uncle Claude can't resist a final insult. "Barnacle!"

The door slams behind Uncle Finn.

Now we are alone.

3

THE HOUSE SEEMS like the emptiest place in the world now that both Marisol and Uncle Finn are gone. And the coldest. It really seems like the actual temperature of the house has gone down ten degrees since their departure.

It's half past ten and we should be asleep. But how can Henry and I sleep at a time like this, stuck in a house with a killer?

I had first thought that Terri and Claude were simply annoying and that Terri shopped too much. That wasn't the kindest notion, and I had vowed to myself to try to keep an open mind, to try to see them with an open heart.

I could laugh at myself now, or cry, for my naïveté. What a simpleton! What a fool!

"We have to do something." Henry's voice breaks the silence, the two of us in our respective beds, staring up at the ceiling, the moon cutting across the rafters.

"I know. But what? I mean . . . no one is going to believe us. They'll think we are paranoid imbeciles."

"Dumb kids who have watched too many movies," he adds.

As we ponder in silence, there's a slow wafting through the room. First a sense, then a movement, ever so slight, then a wave of dusty blue. The wave starts to take shape, languidly, in time. And now Henry and I stare at the forms of our ancestor ghosts, coalescing across the room. Little by little they arise from the dusky smoke.

"What do ya think? This was Maxine's idea. Of course. This soupy one." Plum gestures to the slate-blue fog. "It gives you plenty of . . . warning, if that's the right word. You like it?"

"Wait. You mean like the wafting blue smoke thing?" I ask.

"Yup. That's right. What do ya think?" Beaumont leans in. "If you ask me it's just plain boring. No pizzazz!"

"Oh please, not everything has to be subtle as a hammer," Maxine defends herself. "I thought the children, being rather sophisticated, would appreciate a little artifice."

"Quite right, quite right." August and Sturdevant nod in approval.

"Welp, how's the mystery going, kiddos? You solve it yet?" Plum asks brightly.

Henry and I share a glance. "Oh, we solved it. It's just that we kind of don't know what to do. No one is gonna believe us, basically," I admit.

"Hamlet," Maxine purrs from the corner.

We all turn to her.

"Ham-what?" That's Beaumont, of course.

"Ah, the Dane!" August and Sturdevant chirp.

"See here! I don't see nothing here to do with dogs!" Again, Beaumont.

"A play within a play." Maxine grins, the cat that ate the canary. "'The play's the thing wherein I'll catch the conscience of the King . . .'"

Henry and I look at each other.

August speaks. "If you don't think anyone will believe you . . ."

". . . allow the proper people to put the pieces together themselves," Sturdevant finishes.

We contemplate this strategy.

"That's exactly right," Henry realizes. "Thank you all so—"

But when we turn back around, excited, they're gone. Nothing. Zero. Zilch. Now we are just having a conversation with the wall.

"Ugh! They keep doing that!" I look at him. "Totally annoying."

We stare ahead at the walnut-paneled wall. The wood creaks a bit in the wind and the two of us suddenly remember we are trapped in this house on the cliff with a murderer.

"Whatever happens"—Maxine's voice echoes from some great unseeable distance—"we aren't far away."

4

"A PLAY WITHIN a play." I turn to Henry, who is sitting criss-cross applesauce in the middle of his teepee, looking pensive. "Do you think it will work?"

He ponders. "Well, it might possibly work to get Uncle Claude to feel guilty, and even possibly *look* guilty. But the question is . . . who will be there to see it? I mean, it's not like the entire coast of California is going to come see some dumb play a couple of kids put on."

Huh. I hadn't thought of that.

"Okay, okay . . . I know . . . what if we give them some incentive. Like we make it some kind of fabulous event . . . ?"

Henry squints. "Perhaps a charitable event. The kind Mom

and Dad would host. In combination with something in-triguing . . ."

"I've got it!" I hop off the ground, excited. "We'll do a super-fantastic movie night . . . some really cool movie screen-ing of a film everyone loves . . . and we'll do it on the lawn. Outside. With the ocean in the back! Remember when Mom threw you that *Star Wars* party, when you were five? Where those Jedi-trainer guys came and we all had to do that treasure hunt for the light sabers and then learn how to be Jedis?"

"Of course. Mom played the *Star Wars* theme when they put the Jedi medal on me." He smiles wistfully.

"Mom really knew how to throw a party." And now I am wistful, too.

We both just sit there a moment, lost in those idyllic days not so long ago.

"But, see, Henry. We'll do it like Mom! We'll throw a big crazy party, with a movie screening on the lawn for a really good cause."

"Mom and Dad did have lots of charitably minded friends," Henry says. "And they do feel badly for us. The power of guilt is very strong . . ."

"We'll dedicate all donations to something truly important, like Feed the Children. I think Dad and Mom would be proud. Oh, and . . . *and* . . . I have all the addresses we need from all those fancy invites to Mom! The ones I hid from Terri."

I run to the box of invitations. There must be at least a

hundred by now. As I'm talking, I *flip, flip, flip* through the stack. "You're not even going to believe the best part. Not even when I show you." I hold up two envelopes. One is an invitation to the Police Officers' Ball. The other is a benefit for Judge Maya Selenator.

"These are from the chief of police and the chief judge in our county."

I nod. "Aka 'the fuzz.' Apparently no charity, ever, edits its guest list."

Henry raises his eyebrows. I know what he's thinking. Suddenly, this plan is seeming very, *very* promising. "So, charity event. Movie screening. Do you think we should do the dastardly play within the play beforehand?"

"Yes!" I nod. "We'll do, like, a fun little play thing before the main event . . . the people who we need to be here will be here. We'll do the play, Claude will freak. Cops will arrest him. Boom."

"Not bad," Henry says. "It might actually work . . ."

"Woo hoo!" I tackle Henry, which is something I haven't done in a while but is something I used to do on a regular basis. The key is to hit below the waist. He doesn't always like it.

"Ugh, Eva, stop! You're so weird!"

"Weird like awesome? Or weird like super awesome?" I joke.

But he's smiling now.

There's nothing better in life than having a plan.

Everything is thrilling now.

Full of possibility!

"Okay, so what movie?" I wonder. "It has to be something people will want to come see. What's a classic movie everybody loves but maybe hasn't seen a million times . . . ?"

"*Casablanca?*"

"Too on the nose."

"*The Discreet Charm of the Bourgeoisie?*"

"Too obscure," I object.

"Okay." And then he thinks of it. "*Touch of Evil*! Orson Welles!"

I take this in. "Orson Welles does have quite a history here in the Central Coast."

"And . . . *and* . . . it involves finding out the guilt of someone, so, theoretically, it has something to do with our underlying diabolical plan." Henry is up on his feet now. We jump around like two overexcited lima beans. Yes, it's been a while since we've felt this. This something like hope.

Maybe we are trapped in a ghost-filled house with a murderer and his girlfriend. But it is also true that there is a way out.

Don't linger on the problem. We are all about the solution.

5

HENRY AND I are sitting on the back porch now, having our lunch. We are eating some extremely unsatisfying sandwiches made with almond butter and organic blackberry jelly on twelve-grain toast. Yes, I made these. Yes, they're terrible.

"Okay." I return the subject to our Machiavellian plan. "So— we do a play within a play, where we *act out* what Uncle Claude did to our parents, *in* the play. Then, when Uncle Claude freaks out, riddled with guilt, which he will because he's *so* guilty, everybody will *see* that he's guilty . . . the cops arrest him."

"I doubt the police are going to arrest him as a result of theater," Henry quips.

"You're right. But . . . if we lay it out really specifically in the play, so Uncle Claude freaks out badly enough . . . and then the cops *notice* this and take him in for questioning . . . ? Then, we just go to the cops, share our evidence, and *boom* . . . Bob's your uncle."

"Your exclamation is clearly unnecessary." Henry peers out over the grassy slope, the sound of the waves crashing beyond. "Do you really think it will work?"

I shrug. "It's worth a shot. Also, don't you think it would be supremely satisfying to see Uncle Claude totally busted, in front of everyone who's anyone? He'll be humiliated! I mean, I know we're not getting real revenge, because murder is against our ethical code. But it will be just like a tiny sweet morsel of vengeance."

"It would certainly be a sight to behold," Henry says. "All right. But I have one request. I'd like to do my magic act before the performance."

"Your—"

"Eva?" Henry holds his hand up, stopping me. "It's important to me."

I nod. "Okay. Deal."

The back door swings open and there is Terri with about ten department store shopping bags in hand.

"Nothing like a little retail therapy. Right, kids?"

"Yeah, I guess," I answer, looking at Henry. Mom would not approve of this conspicuous consumption.

"You might be interested to know that Eva and I are planning on putting on a play, as well as screening a film, as part of a charity event. Here. At the house. Preferably in the yard. I intend to do my magic act." Henry appears to be swelling with pride.

Terri comes down from the landing. "A play? Well, isn't that sweet."

"Yes, it *will* be sweet." I wink at Henry.

"Well, if you're fixing to do your magic act, then I ought to do my rodeo act!" Terri suddenly drops all the shopping bags in her excitement.

"Are you *serious*?" Whoops. That came out wrong. "I mean . . . wow! Cool! Are you serious?" Enthusiastically.

"You bet. Not only was I in the rodeo, you are looking at the three-year all-state champ of the Arizona Lasso League. Go Big Turquoise!" Terri seems to be turning into a different person.

"Big turquoise?" Henry asks.

"Well, sure. I think that would be great, Terri." I take a moment. "I'd like to thank you for contributing. Henry and I both appreciate it. Very much. Don't we, Henry?" I elbow him.

"Yes. Yes, we do. Thank you for volunteering for this exciting endeavor."

"You'll need to up your practice schedule. We need you ropin' day and night!" I tell her.

"That's no problemo. Aw, shucks. It'll be fun!"

She swats the air, playful, before marching up the stairs, presumably to rest her arms from the weight of all those shopping bags.

Henry watches Terri go. "Nice move, sister."

I nod. "Now she'll be busy roping while we're busy putting a bow on all our plans."

6

WE SHOULD HAVE known that anyone and everyone would be dying to participate in the opening numbers. Terri. *Check.* Random yoga instructor from down the street. *Check.* Bearded Guitar-Playing Guy from local café. *Check.* I've decided to stop even mentioning the talent portion of the evening, as every time I do, someone seems to offer their dazzling, never-before-seen number. Who knew there was so much undiscovered talent around here? Every time I put up a flyer there's a new volunteer. At this rate the show is going to last twenty hours.

Terri seems to have become the default organizer. Somewhere between the newfound return to the lasso, the feeding of hungry children, and the phone ringing off the hook, it's as if Terri the Terrible unzipped her Terri-suit and a new Terri has come popping out. And this Terri is *motivated*.

I am, personally, refraining from performing. I know! So many people will be disappointed! But I've made up my mind. My role in this is to simply keep the show going. I'll do a little announcing, maybe. Other than that? The show must go on!

It's been three weeks from conception to this mystical night of magic. Three *long* weeks. The house has been freezing and, if it weren't for our shindig here, I'm sure Henry and I would have fallen into a deep depression. We haven't seen Uncle Finn. Marisol is still (we think) in Guatemala. So Henry and I have been stuck together like glue, hoping not to run into Uncle Claude on our lonesome.

During the day, he's at the office. At night, we've barricaded ourselves into our room. So far, it's kept us safe.

And now, we're here! In a few minutes it's curtains up. Bearded Guitar-Playing Guy is slated to do an acoustic version of Coolio's "Gangsta's Paradise" from that movie where that blond lady saves all those inner-city kids. I'm not really a fan of the movie but Guitar Guy auditioned for us and he really puts his heart and soul into it.

Before him, Random Yoga Instructor Lady will be doing a traditional Spanish dance involving these clickety-clackety jobbies that she clicks theatrically. The dance is called flamenco but I call it awesome. She kind of squiggles around like a cobra and then stops dramatically, clicking the castanets. Also, she gets to wear this embroidered burgundy-and-black Spanish dress that basically belongs in the Smithsonian Institution. I'm sure by the end of the dance every male in the audience will be throwing himself onto the stage and begging to slay a dragon for her. I don't know Random Yoga Instructor Lady very well, but I will say I'm quite impressed with her.

I haven't seen Terri's lasso routine yet. She says she's saving it for us, but I'm a little concerned that might mean it's horrible. I just hope she doesn't fall off the stage into the audience.

Awkward.

Henry's magic routine tonight consists of turning a bunch of sheets of paper into doves. I haven't actually seen him do the routine, but I have noticed that the toilet paper seems to be running out.

The play within the play is really the pièce de résistance.

I don't want to tell you too much about it, because I don't want to spoil the surprise. Let's just say it would be extremely difficult to sit through if you happened to be named *Claude*.

In case you're wondering, the ticket sales for tonight's big event, i.e., the screening of "*Touch of Evil*—Under the Stars," have skyrocketed. So much so that we have had to actually rent out a bunch of bleachers, hire security, and provide enticing vittles for this menagerie of film aficionados.

Like I said, Terri really threw herself into it.

I've even heard tell there are people coming from both up the coast, aka Santa Cruz, and down the coast, aka Cambria. I don't doubt this because some of these people streaming in are definitely not wearing socks with sandals. Which is a thing we do hard-core here in Big Sur.

Henry has been selling last-minute tickets at the box office we've constructed from hay bales. Why hay bales, you ask? Well, why not. Also, they were originally going to serve as seats until the great bleacher rental.

I'm hoping that the do-it-yourselfness of the whole event comes off as "cute" and not "pathetic disaster the likes of which these cliffs have never seen."

The best part about it is, we are donating all of it, all the ticket sales, etc., to the Children's Food Bank of California, to feed hungry children and their families. So, even though this thing is thrown together on a shoestring, the cause is a worthy one and the atmosphere seems genuinely kind. Positive. We've even been giving out Children's Food Bank flyers and taking donations. There's a giant glass jar next to the box office, in case you want to contribute. Don't be stingy.

"Hello! Are you Eva?" A square-jawed man with closely cropped hair leans down to shake my hand. I would know this man anywhere. He is our most important guest—other than Claude.

"Chief Talley!" I cheer. "So glad to have Monterey County's finest with us tonight!"

The tiny woman next to him beams at me. "It's so wonderful what you kids are doing here." The corners of her eyes sparkle with unspilled tears. "Your mother would be so proud."

I smile and swallow hard against the lump in my throat. "Thank you, um, here! Please take your seats right here, on the aisle. Want the chief to have easy access to the exit in case duty calls!"

The actual stage faces out from the direction of the ocean, so while we wait for the sun to go down, with our enthralling flamenco-slash-lasso-slash-acoustic-slash-magic show, the audience can relax with their refreshing refreshments and admire the giant orange sun dipping itself into the Pacific Ocean. Not bad, huh? That part was Terri's idea, too.

The giant curtain we patched together from a bunch of old quilts, sails, and blankets is covering the stage, so as to preserve the mystery before the big reveal!

Back in the house, Random Yoga Instructor Lady is practicing her moves, Bearded Guitar-Playing Guy is warming up his voice in a manner I find humorous but he seems to be taking quite seriously, and Terri is in the bedroom, hopefully, please God, hopefully, practicing.

And where is Claude, you might ask?

There. Down center stage three rows back. The sweet spot. Not only, as Henry declared, are the acoustics best in these particular seats, but he will be up close, real close, to see his heinous crime demonstrated for all to see.

Shame! Shame! they will say.

In my mind, they also hurl tomatoes, but nobody has brought tomatoes. I notice there are, however, cherry tomatoes on the bruschetta, so they could carefully be picked off and thrown with abandon.

There's a long line of cars down the access road, which actually turns right into Pacific Coast Highway. Oh, and the *Monterey Herald* did a little piece on the "two tragically orphaned kids," aka us, "who are trying to make the world a better place." So, that helped.

As the sky starts to turn lavender above, there's a kind of anticipation in the air. The little candles and solar lights Henry rigged up all over the place are starting to show themselves a bit now, with the loss of the light, twinkling. He put about a zillion of these lights everywhere, even though I told him he was going too far, but he said it was a purposeful aesthetic choice and that magicians were also artists.

Whatever.

Suddenly, from out in the audience, I catch someone smiling at me and waving madly. It's Uncle Finn!

A rush of warmth comes over me.

The last time we saw him, when Uncle Claude kicked him out, was about three weeks ago. Honestly, I thought he'd be in Timbuktu by now.

I wave back at him in enthusiastic spurts. Uncle Finn came. He came to support us. I call over to Henry, who is busying himself with the last-minute magician pre-show touches.

"*Psst!* Henry! Look, it's Uncle Finn! Finn's here!"

Henry looks up at me blankly, follows my gaze, and sees Uncle Finn. He smiles, waves, and looks back at me.

Uncle Finn gives us a double thumbs-up. He is proud. Beaming.

Out of the corner of my eye, I see Random Yoga Instructor Lady sneak back behind the makeshift curtain, flamenco dress billowing in the breeze. A few members of the audience catch her, too, and there's an audible gasp. The hive mind seems to realize the show is about to begin. The anticipation is palpable. The spotlight comes up on the curtain. A hush falls over the bleachers and somewhere down the driveway, a mockingbird tries to steal the show.

Something's going to be stolen tonight, all right. The freedom of one horrible person: Claude Billings the Third.

7

SOMETHING STRANGE HAPPENS during the flamenco
cobra dance. Behind, on the screen that will eventually show
the long-lost movie, a set of a thousand stars appears. The hyp-
notizing stars twinkle and glow and I find myself amazed that
Henry was able to put this production design together. I guess
he really *is* an artist. The audience oohs and ahhs, not just at
the flamenco dance, with its winding snake moves and castanet
clicking, but at the sheer spectacle of this enchanting dance in
front of the enchanting stars. It's like a magic spell.

When Random Yoga Instructor Lady finishes the dance with
a dramatic swoop, one hand in the air and a rose in her hair,
the audience rises to its feet. Everyone hooting and howling,

"Bravo! Perfecto! Encore!"

She smiles and even seems to blush a little as she curtsies, holding out her embroidered dress like an old-timey member of the court. She glides off the stage and now we are left with Bearded Guitar-Playing Guy from the café.

It's a little less successful with him, to be true. He comes up on the stage, sits down humbly on a hay bale, and begins to strum the silky opening chords of "Gangsta's Paradise." At first, it does seem like a soulful ballad and there's hope. Then, it all goes horribly wrong.

Cringe.

It's not just that once the song is revealed his heartfelt singing feels almost like a joke . . . which, by the way, it does. Example: Someone even laughs out loud in the audience before getting elbowed by his wife. And it's not that some members of the audience have a devout attachment to the heartwarming movie about saving inner-city kids with blondness. It's that, for some bizarro reason, he keeps slipping off the hay bale. Now, I don't know about you, but I have never noticed it's particularly hard to sit on a hay bale. Usually, the directions are: 1) See hay bale. 2) Sit on hay bale. 3) Stay. However, Bearded Guitar-Playing Guy maybe didn't practice or is wearing unusually slippery skinny jeans or has lost his ear/brain equilibrium.

Whatever the case may be, he keeps falling over. So, it goes: Strum strum. Sing. Fall. Recover. Strum strum strum. Sing soulfully. Fall. Recover. Rinse and repeat.

The members of the audience are too nice to heckle him, although I do notice a couple of bored husbands holding in their laughter under the watchful eyes of their well-mannered wives. Also, everyone pretends not to hear this from the bleachers:

"Mooooommy, why does he keep faaaaalling?"

Then, the wind kicks up about fifty notches and the screen leans over to approximately a sixty-degree angle, coming dangerously close to blowing over on top of both Bearded Guitar-Playing Guy and the entire audience.

He, then, looks up in horror, ends his song prematurely, and dashes off the stage, slumped over like a hermit. He looks over at me furtively on his way down the stage steps.

I offer an enthusiastic thumbs-up.

There is a smattering of polite applause.

I'm not sure what effect the wind is going to have on Terri's lasso extravaganza, but I am only going to assume that her Arizona state competitions prepared her for inclement weather.

She begins to take the stage. Henry, who is behind the screen preparing his magic act, looks up at me. We share a look of dread.

Oh, Lord. Please help us.

Apparently, our prayers are answered as the wind dies down just as she settles in.

What happens next can only be described as a historic transformation the likes of which we have never seen. Henry stops preparing his magic kit and ducks down behind the speakers, stage left, just to take it in. I find myself walking forward in a kind of trance. And the audience—you could hear a grain of sand drop to the floor.

Terri takes the stage with gravitas, standing in the middle of the pitch black under a lone spotlight. She's wearing an all-black Western outfit, with stitching and mother-of-pearl buttons, slick pants, and cowboy boots with snakes twisting up the sides, sinister. The whole getup somehow manages to look regal, tailored, elegant. From somewhere behind her, a sad, soulful song plays. From below the stage, a fog begins to rise. Under the lights it climbs around Terri like a thousand serpents. She stays perfectly still. The audience holds its breath.

And then . . . it begins.

The lasso comes up, suddenly in a circle twirling outside of her, and around her, and beside her, then around again. In little circles, and then big circles, and then giant circles. So giant you'd think she couldn't possibly keep control. And then the lasso is miraculously transformed into a whip, and then suddenly the whip is cracking, twirling, spinning around, and Terri is cracking the whip to the beat of the dramatic song. Each crack of the whip on the stage drawing a gasp from the crowd.

But that's not all, no, sir.

Before we know it, Terri magically lights the lasso *on fire.* So now she is twirling, essentially, a ring of fire in front of her, in back of her, side to side. The audience erupts into spontaneous applause, whistling and cheering all around. Whooping and hollering.

The wailing song crescendos and now Terri does the

unthinkable. She jumps in the middle of the ring of fire, spinning it in circles around her body. Now she jumps in. Now she jumps out again. Now in. Now out again.

And here . . . for her grand finale, she actually spins the rope from her ankles below, up up up around her, the fire spinning around her like a blazing tornado, and up over her head. One. Two. Three times! And then she majestically spins the lasso out with a flourish. *Whoosh!* No more fire.

Done.

There is a moment of stunned silence as the song comes to an abrupt end.

And then it's like chaos.

The entire crowd leaps to its feet—pictures, flashes, hoots, hollers, communists are marrying libertarians in the aisles. The spotlight comes back up and Terri stands there, proud. Beaming. The light reflecting off her face, radiant, her breath coming in and out, fast. Like a Western goddess she stands there taking it in. Flush.

She is amazing!

And I will never call her Terri the Terrible again.

This applause lasts for a good five minutes. Then Terri comes off the stage and gives me a wink, descending the steps.

Well, well.

Who knew?

Henry awkwardly mounts the stage.

"Honestly, I'd like to direct you all to lower your expectations immediately."

He says this with all sincerity but the audience laughs.

"I'm serious. This is going to be a grind, unfortunately, compared to the prior act."

And the lights come down and now the screen behind Henry is filled with twinkling stars, which seem to almost come off the screen, the clouds from the screen seem to go from two dimensions to three, wafting upward and outward to mix with the fog coming up from beneath the stage. I'll say this, Henry has really outdone himself with these special effects. I mean, they look like something you'd see at Disneyland. Or, possibly, Universal Studios, where they happen to have a Harry Potter section complete with rides, but no I don't want to go, stop asking me.

As discussed, this magic routine involves turning common paper towels into doves. At first one dove, then two, then three, then four, and on and on until I find myself not only wondering how, exactly, Henry is accomplishing this feat but, also, *Where the heck did he get all those doves?* By the end of the routine, I count about fifty doves, which seems impossible considering I have no idea where they even came from.

I imagine myself caring for fifty doves for the rest of my life.

I will have to build them an aviary and find the proper foliage.

Before I know it, the routine is over and the applause is authentically enthusiastic. No, it wasn't quite the showstopper Terri's flaming lasso routine was but, let's be honest, nothing could be. Had I known, I would have put Terri last in the lineup. That's showbiz.

Henry comes off the stage and gives me a nod.

"Ready, sis?"

And my stomach fills with butterflies. Here it is, folks. The moment of truth.

The play within the play.

(Yes, I'm terrified.)

But there is, also, the small detail of justice. Justice for my parents.

I manage to sneak a look at Uncle Claude in the crowd.

He's tilting back a drink, joking around with his neighbor.

And he will never see this coming.

8

TO SAY THAT Henry put a lot into the play within the play does not do it justice. Quite simply, he spent all last week cutting the scenery, finding a boat off Craigslist, and building a miniature Queen Mary Victorian home out of gingerbread. Bearded Guitar-Playing Guy has agreed to play the part of Uncle Claude, dressed in a kind of suburban-man outfit. Light blue oxford. Beige khakis. The parts of both myself and Henry will actually be played by miniature figurines, created by Henry from his super-nerdy Dungeons & Dragons collection. There is a series of projected texts on the back screen as well, everything from e e cummings to Shakespeare. Also, we have moody and evocative background music, which Henry has also been noodling over for weeks.

There's a pretty simple structure to this little piece of theater. Act I: We are happy, everything's great. Act II: Claude shows up, sees the house, gets greedy, plants a bomb on the boat, removes the life jackets. Act III: Our parents, played by Henry and me, go out on the boat, which explodes, and sink to the bottom of the ocean whilst the music crescendos and the billowing smoke blows in. Then, Uncle Claude, played by Bearded Guitar-Playing Guy, steals the Queen Anne Victorian gingerbread house, all the while cackling maniacally.

Do not, folks, be fooled by the simplicity of the plot. The music, combined with the projections and the fog, all contribute to turning this rather rudimentary tale into a mixed-media theatrical *experience*. I don't want to toot my own horn, obviously, but I think it's rather inspired.

Lastly, our lines are projected onto the screen behind us, à la silent film, so that Henry and I are able to embody our respective characters. I forgot to mention, as a final bit of flair for the dramatic, Henry has decided we should be wearing masks, so he's created two papier-mâché masks in our parents' likenesses that are somehow much more interesting than our own actual faces. Bearded Guitar-Playing Guy didn't want to wear his Uncle Claude mask, but we finally convinced him it was an aesthetic choice and we needed consistency among the characters.

By the end of the first act, everyone is clapping wildly. Henry and I hold for the audience, exiting backstage as our castmate goes onstage as Uncle Claude.

"I think they really like it," I whisper into Henry's ear.

"It appears so."

"Can you see Uncle Claude in the audience?" I ask.

"Yes, so far he looks very much involved. I'm not sure he realizes that's supposed to be him onstage."

"Not yet," I whisper back.

I'm fairly sure when Uncle Claude does realize it, his face will go from vague amusement to crimson indignation.

Bearded Guitar-Playing Guy, dressed as Uncle Claude, boards the boat and plants the prop TNT at the helm. The audience watches with keen interest. Tension in the air.

Now he tiptoes off the stage, taking off his mask behind the curtain.

"How was I? Do I seem convincing as a suburban man?"

"Yes, you were brilliant!" I answer.

Now Henry and I scurry back onto the stage, as our parents, seating ourselves back in the boat. We mimic the boat's movement through the water by projecting moving water on the screen behind us. Pretty sneaky, huh?

It's a moment of quiet serenity. No music. Calm. Peaceful. Then . . .

BOOM!

The special-effects explosion rocks the stage. A simple mixture of ammonia and bleach. Henry was really excited putting that whole business together. The audience gasps. A few people let out a sigh of relief and a nervous laugh.

Henry and I, in our masks, mimic falling into the ocean by lying down ever so slowly, with silk chiffon ribbons of different shades of blue waving all around us, standing in for the deep blue sea.

The audience grows nearly silent.

You could hear a pin drop.

You see, many of the people here know us. They know our story. They know about our parents' deaths. And now they know that our little play is a bit more profound, meaningful, and pointed than perhaps they had imagined.

The atmosphere is *heavy*. You could cut the air up with a butter knife right now.

Henry and I sneak off the stage and now the Uncle Claude actor comes back on, in his Uncle Claude mask.

But now, the *actual* Claude, in the audience, is starting to shift in his seat. He looks around at the people near him but no one dares to look back.

As the Uncle Claude actor cackles madly from the stage and begins stealing the miniature Victorian gingerbread house, wheeling it away . . . the *real* Claude, our uncle, finally cracks.

"Enough! Enough! Lights! Lights! Turn on the lights!" he bellows, standing up from his seat in the audience.

Henry rushes over to the lighting equipment and turns the spotlight on Uncle Claude and Uncle Claude only. He stands there, cursing and holding his arm over his eyes to shield himself from the white-hot spotlight and the stares of the entire audience. A deer in headlights.

We got him.

We got him good.

As the audience begins to whisper, point, cover their mouths, and whisper again, the chief of police swaggers his way over to Uncle Claude.

"Claude, kind of looks like something might have struck a nerve here tonight," Chief Talley says, sizing him up.

More hushed whispers from the rest of the audience, furtive glances.

"Officer, I just . . . I can't believe what's happening here. This is insane! This is crazy!" Uncle Claude laughs nervously, looking around him at the rest of the audience.

"Well, that may be. But you're causing a disturbance. So maybe you should come with me and just answer a few questions. If you don't mind, sir," the cop suggests.

Claude looks around him at the accusatory glances, from every direction. Surrounded. Caught.

"Don't you people see? This is a setup! I'm an innocent man!"

Somehow the more he says it, the less true it seems. Some members of the audience look away now, ashamed for him. I don't blame them. It's painful.

Uncle Finn watches from his seat in the audience.

Terri watches from the opposite side of the stage.

"Terri?" Uncle Claude looks to her, pleading. She averts her eyes, looking down at the ground, troubled.

Now Claude looks back to the audience, to his brother, Finn, for salvation. "Aren't you going to stop them? This is madness!"

But Uncle Finn only looks on with pity in his eyes, giving a slight shake of the head, stunned.

"All right, sir. No need for hysterics. We just want to ask a few questions. That's all." The police officer has had enough.

"No, I absolutely refuse. No. I will not." Uncle Claude stops short of stamping his feet.

"Sir, you may want to come down with us, right now, in a voluntary fashion."

"This is ridiculous!"

And now the police officer is losing patience. He leans in and whispers, "Mr. Billings, we can do this the civilized way or the ugly way. It's up to you. May I remind you there are children present." The officer nods over to me and Henry, staring from beside the stage.

Uncle Claude looks over at us.

A moment of contemplation.

He nods at the officer, dutifully, and the two of them come quietly down from the bleachers. A fellow officer joins them on the way out. It looks a lot like they're heading for the police station.

For a moment, no one knows what to do. Is it over? What about the screening? Is everything ruined?

I leap onstage and make an announcement.

"Okay. Ladies and gentlemen, thank you for being patient. Now let's all just take a breath, sit back, relax, and watch the film we came here to see!"

There's an audible sigh of relief.

I come off the stage toward Henry.

We share a moment.

"Holy moly! We did it. We actually did it," I say, breathless.

"Do you think Mom and Dad would be proud of us?"

"What? Of course they would be!"

Up on the screen, the film begins. Twenty feet tall, black and white, through the streets and over the arches of the beginning of *Touch of Evil*.

Henry smiles at me, somehow lost in thought.

Our nightmare is finally over.

9

THE AUDIENCE IS still rapt as Henry and I make our way behind the giant flickering image to the box office. We saw that justice was done, *and* raised money for hungry children. That feels right, giving back something.

The Random Yoga Instructor Lady and the Bearded Guitar-Playing Guy have taken a seat next to each other in the audience, staring up at the celluloid and all the dreams thrown on it.

We're about halfway behind the screen when Henry stops short.

"Hey, you almost tripped me!"

"Shh. Eva. Stop."

Henry is standing there like a cat with his spine up, perfectly still. The ions around him charged.

I freeze behind him, puzzled. It takes everything I have not to open my mouth, but there's something swirling around my kid brother that I know not to mess with. Something electric.

Instead, I try to figure out what, exactly, is his damage. He's staring past the screen, about fifty yards away, and at first, I can't quite tell what he's looking at.

But then I look closer.

It's Uncle Finn.

And closer still.

Oh *no*!

Have you ever been in a car crash? Even a little one? You know that feeling where time slows down and everything seems like it's taking three hours but it's really only three seconds? As if the very nature of time is stretched out like Silly Putty?

That's this moment.

Staring at Uncle Finn.

And I can't believe what I see.

10

HENRY STAYS NEXT to me, still as a statue, the giant image of Orson Welles projected behind him.

Uncle Finn's movement is hurrying, a furtive kind of thing.

It's the movement of someone putting. Putting one thing from here to there. But what is it? What is he doing?

And then it comes into focus and I see exactly what it is. There, in big black Sharpie letters that are very familiar to me because I scrawled them out earlier, in a rush:

CHILDREN'S FOOD BANK

And the putting?

Finn is taking money out of the labeled Children's Food Bank jar and putting it into something.

BANG!

Like dynamite, it hits me.

It hits me straight in the gut.

The money is being put into Uncle Finn's pocket.

And that is Finn's own hand, doing the putting.

"Finn?"

It comes out of me before I can stop it. A question mark.

Uncle Finn looks up, caught, his hand in the donation jar.

"Oh, hi there. I was just making sure we had all the donations and, uh, I—"

"What are you doing, Uncle Finn?" Suddenly I feel like
Little Cindy Lou Who, catching the Grinch.

"Me? Oh, nothing. It's just I was keeping these safe for you.
I was going to take them back to that little inn down the way
and—"

"That little inn," Henry says, his tone flat. "The one with
the good breakfast."

Uncle Finn smiles. "Yes, exactly!"

"How did you know about the breakfast at that inn? You
never visited us before. And you said you came straight to our
house the minute you found out Mom and Dad had died."

Uncle Finn chuckles. "Now, buddy, I—"

"And the farm workers' wages. You said you read about
them when you were scolding Terri about her spa expenses. But
that was in the paper—" I stop. I can't believe what I'm about to
say—"the same week Mom and Dad died."

"It was *you*." This comes out of Henry.

Uncle Finn stands still, smiling weakly.

"It was you, all along." Henry has turned to stone now.

"What?" Uncle Finn yelps. "Whattayou, whattayou mean, are you—"

And now it all comes to me, in a kind of memory montage from start to finish, but all things at once.

Uncle Finn showing up in our lives out of nowhere.

Uncle Finn hating Claude with a burning passion.

Uncle Finn having one of his *many* degrees in chemistry.

Uncle Finn inheriting the house, once Claude is locked up.

Uncle Finn finding that key inside the boathouse.

And, finally, Uncle Finn . . . *planting that miniature wooden box in Uncle Claude's armoire.* That's why it didn't make sense in the first place. Why on earth, if Claude was the killer, would he keep around that completely incriminating small wooden box? The answer is . . . he wouldn't. The answer is . . . he didn't. The answer is . . . Uncle Finn planted it there.

All to get the house.

He pretended to be the coolest guy in the world and our one and only trusted friend and confidant.

When, all along . . .

It was him.

11

BEFORE I KNOW what to do, or say, or why the earth revolves around the sun, Uncle Finn makes a mad dash, out over the green toward the cliffs, out away from the crowd. The black-and-white screen flickers behind him, turning him into a kind of strobe runaway.

Henry bursts out after him, an uncharacteristic show of athleticism, to be honest. I take off after Henry after Uncle Finn. Behind us, twenty-foot Orson Welles wants nothing to do with us.

Uncle Finn must have run track-and-field in high school because we are almost starting to lose him in the marine layer, coming up from the sea, slowly enveloping the cliffs.

Henry and I try to catch up, panting.

What does he think he's going to do, dash into the sea? The cliff edge is mere feet away.

"Finn! Uncle Finn! Stop!!" I yell it out into the grayish pea soup creeping up over the precipice. "Henry, he's gonna kill himself! We have to stop him!"

I'm not sure Henry had thought of that. I think he was a little more focused on the fact that our uncle Finn was just caught red-handed stealing money from impoverished starving children and, also, therefore, revealing himself to be the unscrupulous con man who killed both our mother and father.

And the worst kind of con man. The one we believed in. The one we trusted. The one we thought was our friend.

"Uncle Finn, stop! Stooooooppppp!!"

Through the billowing dusty gusts, we can see him, right there, poised over the cliff, teetering!

He turns to us.

"It's too late. It's too late, kids. Stay back!"

Henry and I slow down, keeping our distance, not wanting to startle him into a fifty-foot drop.

"It's not too late! It's never too late. Please, Uncle Finn," I beg.

As mad as I am right now, I do not want the death of anyone on my conscience. No way.

Henry has clearly delegated the role of crisis counselor to me. That's okay. He does tend toward putting his foot in his mouth in intense situations. And this, mind you, is the most intense situation he and I have ever been in.

Uncle Finn is turned to us, barely able to look us in the eye.

"I blew it, kids. I blew up my life. I screwed up everything. And then I thought I had this shot, this one shot, and look at you, look at the two of you, you beautiful, kind, generous kids. No. I can't live with myself. I just can't."

He turns back toward the cliffs, his swan song over the sea.

"No! We forgive you. Don't we, Henry? We forgive you. We really do." I attempt a truce.

He stops for a second.

"You do?"

"*Yes!* We do. But if you jump off that cliff, Uncle Finn, you will never get a chance to forgive yourself."

Uncle Finn squints at us through the fog.

Oh, please God.

Did I say the right thing?

This silence is killing me.

And then.

He steps away from the cliff.

He steps backward and puts his head in his hands, caving in on himself.

"I'm so sorry. I'm so, so sorry."

Henry and I look at each other.

Our parents taught us. Mercy. And forgiveness.

Henry and I step carefully forward, and then forward again, nearing Uncle Finn.

Now, just a step away, we reach out to embrace this pathetic sight, this grown man sobbing to himself on the edge of the abyss.

And it's a beautiful moment. A picture-perfect moment. A moment to be proud.

Except.

Uncle Finn swoops up the two of us, like fish on a line, and hangs us, dangling one in each arm, smack-dab over the perilous cliff.

"Oh, you poor, naïve little suckers."

12

FIFTY FEET BELOW us the waves smash into the side of the cliffs, the salty mist coming up from the treacherous white waves. Looking down, beneath my dangling feet, there is only air now, nothing to shield us from the rocks and the brine.

Henry is yelling out, "Help! Mayday, Mayday!"

But Uncle Finn puts an end to that. "One more word and I drop your sister."

Henry looks at me, cowed.

"You kids are so dumb. Little Miss Perfect over here, and Nerd of the Century. You have no idea what the world is like. The wolves at the gate."

I'm saying a prayer in my head right now. It's not much, but I'm just going impromptu, praying for Henry and me to somehow survive, praying that if we die, we will join Mom and Dad. God, Jesus, Buddha, Yahweh. Any takers. I'm sure Henry is praying to the great programmer in the sky. A kingdom in heaven of ones and zeroes.

"What little fools you are! What a sad little pair of orphans you make! Your parents raised you so very soft. Soft like little-itty baby sheep. Baa. Baa." And now he is laughing, laughing and bleating, crazed. "Baaaaaa. Ha ha! Baaaaaa!"

Clearly, Uncle Finn is not who we thought he was. Now that I think about it, he's just plain off his nut.

I turn to my brother. "Henry . . . I love you."

It's almost impossible to hear me over the waves below.

"You're the best kid brother anyone could have."

My eyes are welling up now. I can't stop thinking of every moment since they brought him home from the hospital, that blue-and-white baby blanket with little bears on it, his very first steps and how we all cheered him on, the first word he said, how he looked up and said "Meat guy" as we passed a McDonald's on the freeway. Every little baby step, every little coo, every little first moment of anything ever, my kid brother, dangling there over the murderous cliff.

"I love you, too, Eva. I love you so much."

That's definitely the first time he's ever said that. Then, this is the first time we've ever been dangled over a cliff.

Down below, an especially behemoth wave torpedoes down into the rocks.

"Oh, how sweet. Two little sheep at death's door. Don't

worry. I'll pray for your little sheep souls. Baah. Baaah. Ba—"

FWAP!

FWOOP!

FWAP!

Everything goes black.

I'm pretty sure I just died.

SO FAR THE afterlife is pretty dark in general. I really thought there was going to be some kind of white-light tunnel involved. And ancestors everywhere.

This? Is very disappointing.

I don't see my mom and dad anywhere.

Maybe they didn't know I was coming.

Oh, okay, *there's* the glowing white light. I can see it now. Just a pinprick but getting bigger. I'll just wait here until it gets big enough for me to step through and then shuffle off this mortal coil and get back to business. I have a list of people I'd like to talk to: Nikola Tesla. Amelia Earhart. Martin Luther King Jr. Cleopatra. Also, a list of people I have some follow-up questions for: Thomas Jefferson. Napoleon. Marilyn Monroe.

If that light would just get a little bigger now I'll just break on through to the other side and start my investigating.

But the light really isn't getting bigger. Not at all. And there's some kind of noise coming in from the sidelines. Indecipherable. But definitely not the sound of Gabriel's trumpet. And no pearly gates. Not even a pearly fence.

"Eva? Evaaaa? Can you hear me?"

Somehow the glowing white light is moving around now and getting really large, blinding me.

"Eva, can you see this?"

I open my eyes, which I didn't necessarily realize were closed, and see an extremely powerful flashlight pointed at my face.

There's a gasp from somewhere, but I just died, so I'm still figuring it out.

"Eva! Eva! Oh my God! You're okay! She's okay! You're okay!"

And there, above me, is my kid brother, Henry, hugging me and gushing in a way I never knew he could gush.

"Oh, Eva. You're all right. You're all right!"

And now I look at the arm holding the flashlight. Yeah, that's definitely a police officer's arm. Definitely a police officer's badge.

But this doesn't seem like heaven, because, honestly, it's pretty dark and I can feel the salt air from the ocean on my cheeks.

"We best get these two kids to a hospital, better safe than

sorry. They must be freezing."

Somewhere far in the distance, behind the screen, I see blue and red lights flashing. Whirring around in circle after circle.

"What? What's that?" I ask.

"That?" Henry follows my eyes. "Oh, that. Well, dear sister. That happens to be our uncle Finn. In handcuffs. In the back of a 2016 Buick LeSabre."

"Wait. What? What happened?"

The cop and Henry give each other a look. Then they both nod in the same direction. I look over.

And there she is.

Terri.

Oh my God.

Terri the Terrible saved our lives?

"Seriously? How?"

She steps up, almost embarrassed. "I sure don't know what happened, kids. I was standing there, one minute, gathering up my lassos. And then it was like . . . well, this sounds crazy but . . . it was like someone, some thing, just *whoooosh*, just turned me around. Like it turned my whole body. And I saw you there, the two of you, with your feet dangling over the cliff and that horrible, hairy man hanging you over the side like urchins. And, well, I thought . . . not on my watch!"

"She lassoed us." Henry smiles, excited. "Can you imagine? Terri lassoed us by the feet and threw us back, back to safety."

The cop adds in, "With both hands. Like a real pro." He smiles at Terri.

"Aw." Terri blushes.

"And then, Eva. You're never going to believe it. She lassoed Uncle Finn right off his feet!" Henry exclaims.

The officer nods in agreement. "It was quite a feat. Heck, I couldn't have done it."

"So . . . I didn't die?" I'm still a little foggy.

"Ha! No, of course not, you little duck." Terri actually hugs me.

I don't think Terri's ever hugged me before.

All this warmth is dampened by the fact that I suddenly realize the horrible, unacceptable, unforgivable thing we did to Uncle Claude. In front of everybody.

"Oh my God. What about Uncle Claude? Is he in jail? We have to save him before someone shanks him!"

The policeman chuckles.

"Well, little missy, I'm pretty sure he couldn't have made it to the station before this got called in. Heck, you may even see him tonight."

"Really?"

"Yeah, really. Clearly, that one in the squad car is the problem. Most people don't go around dangling kids off a cliff. Not in my experience."

I look at Henry. "God, I feel terrible. We were such idiots!"

"Indeed." Henry nods.

"No," Terri tells us, "you kids are the smartest kids I've ever known. No one—not *anyone*—suspected that something had happened to your folks *on purpose*. But you did. How did you ever figure it out?"

Henry and I look at each other, then turn to the family graveyard up the hill. "Call it a hunch," Henry says with a shrug.

The blue and red lights circle round on top of the car. Uncle Finn is driven up the driveway, hopefully never to be seen again.

Marisol was right.

Never trust a man who doesn't do anything.

14

IT'S NEARLY TWO in the morning and Claude still hasn't returned, but neither Henry nor I have any intention of going to sleep. In fact, Terri, Henry, and I are waiting patiently in the living room, a fire blazing in the fireplace. We've even put on music to make it seem like a real warm welcome.

We have a lot to make up for.

"Terri, there's really no way to thank you for—"

"Oh, kids. Don't wax poetic. I got it." She swats away our gratitude.

"Honestly, Terri, we really have to—"

"You want to know what, kids? You may think I saved you and, well, of course, I did. But . . . putting on that show, rehearsing, getting back to the lasso, I realized something."

Henry and I listen, warmed by the flicker of the fire.

"When I was younger, I just loved the rodeo. And I was good at it. But somewhere along the line, someone decided I was pretty. And then next thing I knew, I was in pageants, doing the lasso for the talent part. And then it was just about pageants. Just about being pretty. And then I was getting older, and less pretty. And then I didn't know who I was, exactly."

Even the flames are listening from the fireplace. Not a crackle.

"And that feeling, the feeling I used to have just being in the moment, the tricks, making them better and better . . . I couldn't get that moment from anything. It was the only time I wasn't restless. And sad."

I get closer to Terri, squeeze her hand for comfort. Her eyes are swelling with tears.

"And now I feel that way again. Thank you," she whispers.

I give Terri a giant hug.

Even Henry comes in for the group embrace.

"I'll call Marisol tomorrow. Find out how she's doing." She dries a lone tear coming down. "She'll be home again soon. And then, maybe we can start all over."

She welcomes our embrace.

The warmth of the fire blazes hot on our backs.

The front door latch turns and there is Uncle Claude, standing in the doorway.

"What is this, some kind of hippie convention?!" he jokes, bellowing.

The three of us disentangle ourselves and look up at him.

Henry and I come forward, tentative.

"Uncle Claude?" I plead. "Can you ever forgive us? We were such idiots. Uncle Finn just bamboozled us . . . every step of the way."

Uncle Claude smiles. "Kids, you would not be the first people that my brother has bamboozled. He left our family because he burned every relationship he had—with me, with your dad, with our parents . . . He burned them to the ground. He lied to us all. He took advantage of the fact that we wanted to believe he was telling the truth. Just like you did."

Henry studies his shoes. "We wanted to believe *you* were the bad guy," he admits. And before I can sock him for being a little too honest, Claude speaks again.

"I think I'm more than a little bit to blame for that. My brother died. And here I was, all of a sudden, with you two and this house to look after. I didn't . . . I didn't want what happened to my brother and your mom to be true. I just threw myself into my work so I wouldn't have to think for a second about your mom and my kid brother . . . They were good people."

There's a giant lump that's formed in my throat. As hard as I try to swallow it down, it won't go away.

Claude continues, "I checked out. And that's on me. It's no wonder you thought I was guilty. I clearly *was* guilty of one thing. Not being here for you kids."

Terri smiles next to us on the couch. "The kids and I were just talking about new beginnings," she says.

"Think I can have some of that crunchy huggy stuff over

here?" Claude asks. He smiles and the four of us go in for an embrace. "Oh, you're killing me. I'm suffocating! This is gross!"

"Uncle Claude, if I may . . . I do have some follow-up questions." Henry looks up at him.

"Go on, shoot."

"Why were you so strange about that condominium diorama? The one at your office."

"Well, because, to tell you the truth, I thought you'd be mad at me. See, that condo complex is going down in San Diego, over the cliffs of a beach, and, quite frankly, there's been a lot of fuss about it. From the bohemian types."

"And you thought we . . ."

"I thought you'd take the side of the hippies. The uh, naked . . . hippies."

Henry and I look at each other.

Beat.

Claude blushes. "It's a nude beach."

And then we burst into laughter.

"Oh my God, naked beach people!" I blurt out. "That was it?!"

And I am shaking my head.

Henry is shaking his head.

"We're so stupid and I hate us right now," I admit.

"Aw, come on, kiddo." Claude ruffles my hair. "All is forgiven! And forgiveness is a—"

"Gift to the giver," Henry and I finish the sentence.

"Now, everyone," he glances at Terri, "it's time for bed. It's been quite a night; don't you think?"

We nod and everybody begins to go their separate ways.

Terri commences to put out the fire, Claude untucks his shirt as he walks up the stairs, letting it all hang out after a long evening of plays, films, cops, and kids.

And Henry?

Well, Henry just walks out the mudroom door and out the back, into the chilled night air.

"Wait! Henry, where are you going?"

"I just, I feel like strolling along for a bit, contemplating, I suppose."

I catch up to Henry on the grass and start walking with him, side by side.

I think about the show we put on. The amazingness of it, before the attempted murder. "You know, those were some effects, Henry. Good job." I pat him on the back.

He turns. "I was just going to say the same to you."

"What?" I respond, puzzled.

We both stop.

"Wait," Henry says. "*You* didn't make the thousands of stars? The light fantastic? The quivering fog?"

"Quivering fog? No! I thought *you* did all that."

"Me! I most certainly did not."

He freezes, looks at me. I think. Then our eyes widen.

"You don't think it was—" We say it together.

This seems to be a kind of cue. Now the wind picks up, driving fast along the hillside, swooping up beside us. There's a kind of massive, vertical swirl around us in blue and plum and violet.

"Heck, I thought you'd never guess!" Beaumont appears, complete with overalls and gold-tinning pan this time.

Beside him Plum appears. "Like it? We wanted to knock your socks off!"

"Like it?! It was incredible!" Henry and I fall all over ourselves. "It was seriously the greatest thing ever."

"Never you mind the flattery; anything for you kids!" Beaumont tilts his hat.

Behind him, August and Sturdevant beam. "It was nothing."

Maxine says in her lilting voice, "Obviously, you can't go wrong with Shakespeare."

"But it was amazing!" I keep on. "It was so beautiful. Breathtaking. How did you do it?!"

"'There are more things in heaven and earth than are dreamt of in your philosophy,'" Maxine purrs.

All five ancestor ghosts grin at each other, pleased and proud. August and Sturdevant raise their martini glasses.

"Here, here. Quite, quite."

"Wait." Henry begins putting it together. "Remember how Terri said someone, or some*thing* just turned her around, all of a sudden, so she saw us on the cliff . . . with Uncle Finn? When he was dangling us over the edge, basically trying to kill us?"

"Yes. I do remember that completely traumatizing experience."

"Eva . . . that was them." He turns to look at Beaumont,

Plum, Maxine, August, and Sturdevant. They face us, brimming. Each of them, in their own way, takes a bow.

Mind. Blown.

Beaumont laughs. "What, you think we're gonna let some slimy, yellow-bellied ne'er-do-well do harm to our kin? No way. No sir. No howdy."

Plum comes forward now, leaning in, gentle. "Listen. You kids ought to know, there's a little surprise for you. Down the cliff."

Henry and I share a look and, before we know it, in the blink of an eye, the five of them are gone, disappeared into the ether. The ghosts of our ancestors. The ghosts of our blood.

Who *saved* us.

A gust of sea air comes up from the ocean, carrying us, and somehow we find ourselves pulled down to the sea, over the path, through the gate, down the slippery stone steps, down below to the bottom of the cliffs. The rocks sticking out of the seabed like a fortress. The full moon hides behind the gray cloud cover, whispering light from behind the bluffs. A secret.

There's a buzzing here. Like the feeling just before it rains.

We stand there, the two of us, listening to the sound of the waves crashing, thinking about how these cliffs, these cliffs we love, and these waves crashing, almost took us with them. Thinking about how we were saved.

And then it happens.

They appear.

There behind the breakers, their figures tiny, gliding gently over the waves, like a kiss.

Mom.

And Dad.

Their figures flicker in and out under the moonlight.

Our mother speaks first.

"Eva . . . Henry." It's almost like a prayer the way she says our names.

Our father comes forward, his eyes welling. "We're so proud of you."

Henry and I can barely control ourselves, seeing the two of them like this. My cheeks are wet with tears and I don't even have to look to know that Henry's are, too.

"How beautiful it was. Your play. It was exquisite."

I'm shaking now. I can barely speak. All I want to do is to jump in their arms and go with them wherever they go. To be with them now and always.

Henry hears my thoughts or thinks them, too.

"Dad? Mom? Does this mean . . . you're staying? Does this mean you're staying here with us?"

It's more of a plea than a question.

For a moment, my mom looks sad, wistful. A look of loves lost.

She looks up at us. My father grabs her hand.

The two of them gaze at us, protective and gentle.

"We can't stay."

I think I hear the sound of our hearts breaking, getting washed away into the sea.

"But, darlings." She tries to be strong. "We're here. We're

always here. With you. Did you know that? We're in everything you see, in the ocean, in the sky, in the stars. Isn't it funny? Love transcends space and time. Love is the thing, the only thing . . . that is infinite."

My father kisses my mother gently on the forehead.

As Henry and I look up at them, they look down with that same look they gave Henry, wrapped in his blue baby blanket, the same look they gave me when I fell off my bike and had to get stitches. Like they wished they could jump in front of everything for us, take every sorrow, slay every dragon.

Keep us safe.

And then they begin to fade. Their figures, like willows, getting softer and softer, while Henry and I hold our breath, wanting to leap into the sky, wanting to go with them.

And then . . . they are gone.

We stand there, the entire world stopped from turning.

Henry reaches out, softly grabs my hand. I grab his.

The two of us together now, against the world.

"Remember what they said, Henry." I can barely breathe, the words getting caught in my throat.

Henry pulls me toward him and the two of us keep each other standing.

Our foreheads are together now, cheeks a stream of tears.

Henry catches his breath and wipes a tear from my eye.

It really is just the two of us now.

"Eva. We just have to remember. If we're love . . ." He raises my chin, gently, looks me in the eye. "Then we get to be infinite."

ACKNOWLEDGMENTS

I would like to thank the people nearest and dearest to me who keep this whole operation running. As most people close to me know, I can write a novel faster than I can fill out a form, so it is quite fortunate I have humans around me who can interact on my behalf. Rosemary Stimola and Kristen Pettit are the two major brilliant forces behind this book. Thank you with all my heart. Now the LA side. I must thank Flora Hackett and Sylvie Rabineau at WME for believing in me, as well as my incredible manager, Sukee Chew. Nothing would be possible without my rabble-rousing husband, Sandy Tolan, as well as my mother, father, sister, and brother. I am so lucky to have such a tight-knit and singular family. I love you all so much. Of course, to my astounding niece and nephew, Eva and Carlitos. And finally, to my darling, illuminating, and effervescent son, Wyatt. You are all the stars in the sky, in the universe, and in the multiverse too. You are infinite.